Love Endures All Things

TERRI SEYMORE-GREEN

Published by Poetry & Prose Publishing, LLC

PUBLISHER'S NOTE

This is a work of fiction. Names, characters, places, and incidents either are a product of the author's imagination or are used fictitiously, and any resemblance to actual persons, living or dead, business establishments, events, or locales is entirely coincidental.

Book cover designed by JD&J with stock imagery provided by HONGQI ZHANG & Michael Simons © 123RF.com

ISBN: 099903300X
ISBN-13: 978-0-9990330-0-5

DEDICATION

To my sons, Brandon and DJ. When I have reached the end of my race, I want the two of you to be able to look back over my life and know that your mother not only found her purpose; but fulfilled it.

CONTENTS

ACKNOWLEDGMENTS

First, I would like to thank my Heavenly Father for giving me the strength to continue the journey I started. I want to acknowledge my cousins, Tammy Seymore Jones who was the first relative to purchase a copy of my first book, *I Love You More Than Love*. For that, I love you dearly. Deidre J. Brown, I thank you so much for introducing me to an opportunity that I might not have otherwise had if it were not for you.

Jeramy Green, I believe you could sell a bikini to an Eskimo in December. Please let your network know, I'm back!

To Dorrie, Andrea H., Nekia, Candy, Felicia, Nicole, Teresa, Marsha, Krystalyn, Tiersa, Tiffany, Tracie, Yvette J., and Teahna, I thank you all for supporting me through my various projects. Donnita, I thank you for the encouraging words you have offered over the past few years regarding fulfilling my passion and living out my purpose. Sometimes when I get discouraged, I refer to them as motivation.

To my sons, Derreck and Brandon. I love and appreciate you both so much. Remember, you can be anything and do anything. You give me the energy to keep going.

Edward "Junie" Henderson, there's so much that I could say about you; but you already know. I appreciate you letting me reach people through you and your events. You have been a Godsend and I will cherish our friendship forever. You're one of the only people who would allow me to stand under your umbrella in a storm. My all-weather friend.

Finally, I want to thank anyone who has had an impact on my life; both negative and positive. I learned how to be greater because of you.

1 THIS IS AN EMERGENCY

Monica got out of her car and headed toward Keisha and Darius's front door. She knocked three or four times then waited for Keisha to answer. *Something's wrong. I just spoke to her an hour ago. She knew I was on my way over.* Standing on the porch, she dialed the house phone but there was no answer. The cell phone went unanswered too. *What in the world is going on?*

"Jamel, it's me," her voice shook with panic. "I just got over to Keisha and Darius's place, but Keisha's not answering. She knew I was on my way over here, so I'm concerned."

"What? Let me call Darius. Maybe she had to run out?" said Jamel.

Monica walked over to the garage. She could clearly see Keisha's BMW through one of the small glass panes. She headed back to the front door to wait for Jamel to return to the line. Resting her back on the frame, the door creaked. It was open.

"Babe, Darius said he talked to her a little over an hour ago. She didn't say anything about going out. In fact, he said she told him you were on your way over there," now Jamel was in a panic too.

"Babe, the door is open. I'm going in. Stay on the line with me, please?" she begged.

"Darius is on his way home. I'm on my way over there too, Monica. Maybe you better wait until I get there before going in."

"What? You know I won't be doing that. My best friend and our Goddaughter might be in trouble. I'm going in now!" she insisted.

"Keisha? Keisha, are you okay?" she took a few steps into the foyer, "Keisha?"

Suddenly, she could hear Keyana crying from her nursery. Monica ran up the stairs and into the baby's room. There was Keyana lying in her crib with her face as red as sunburned skin. Her urine-soaked mattress was an indication of how long she had been there with no one to care for her. Monica scooped Keyana up from the soiled sheets and headed toward Keisha and Darius's room. The comfort of Monica's warm embrace calmed her to a whimper. There on the floor was Keisha. The rise and fall of her back confirmed that she wasn't dead.

"Oh my God, Jamel! I found her! She's unconscious on the bedroom floor!" she screamed while trying to console Keyana at the same time.

Placing the baby in the center of the king-sized bed, she grabbed the house phone from its base and dialed 911.

"Hello, I need an ambulance at 125 Hickory Street in Upper Marlboro! Please hurry!"

"What's the nature of your emergency, Ma'am?" asked the 911 operator.

"My friend is lying on the floor unconscious! Her baby's here and it looks like she's been crying for a while, please hurry!"

"I have someone on the way. What is your name?"

"Monica!"

"Monica, does your friend have a pulse?"

"Yes, she's breathing but that's it. She's unconscious! Keisha? Keisha? Can you hear me?" Monica's voice trembled with fear. "Oh my God! Please hurry."

"What's the baby's name?"

"Keyana! You're asking a lot of questions! Please get someone over here now!"

"Monica, I'm going to have to ask you to calm down. Does Keyana appear to be harmed in any way?"

"No, I don't believe so."

While Monica communicated with the 911 operator, she heard a noise coming from Keisha's closet. She placed the phone on the nightstand and grabbed Darius's gun that was in the drawer. Thrusting the closet door open, she saw a figure dressed in dark clothing hunched in the corner.

"Who in the hell are you? What are you doing here?"

There was no response from the intruder who was still cowering in the corner of the closet. Suddenly, the dark figure lunged toward Monica, grabbing her by the neck. The stranger was no match to Monica's strength. In the background, Keyana began to cry again. The commotion in the closet had startled her. Suddenly, a loud pop rang out from the space within. Keyana's crying intensified. The dark figure fell to the floor gasping for air. Monica snatched the mask from the intruder's face.

"Stephanie! What have you done?"

The sound of sirens began to get closer by the second. Then finally, the room filled with silence. Keyana was no longer crying and there was no movement from Stephanie who was lying motionless on the closet floor. PG County Police and the paramedics raced up the stairs and into the room.

Monica ran back toward the phone. "They're here! I've shot someone!"

"Monica, who is the person you shot?"

"Her name is Stephanie Morgan. She's been stalking this family for over a year now."

"Is she still breathing?"

Monica guided the paramedics to Stephanie's body that was still lying motionless on the closet floor.

"She's dead," one of the paramedics announced. "We're going to need the crime scene unit," he motioned to an officer standing nearby.

"She's dead. I killed her, "Monica confirmed for the 911 dispatcher that Stephanie was gone. "I killed her! I killed her!"

The second paramedic worked on Keisha who was still struggling to breathe. The crime scene investigations unit arrived to work the scene. The investigation revealed ligature marks around Keisha's neck. Stephanie had tried to choke the life out of her. Keisha was a survivor and would prayerfully be okay. Monica had finally put an end to the torture and hell that Stephanie had put the family through for the past fourteen months.

Darius and Jamel arrived one behind the other. Keisha and baby Keyana were both rushed to the hospital.

"Monica! Are you okay?"

"Yes, I'm okay. But I just killed someone. Stephanie is dead!" she cried.

"I'm going with the ambulance. It's okay," he looked to Jamel for reassurance. "It's going to be okay."

Jamel remained by her side, consoling her because she was visibly shaken. In his heart, he worried. What was going to happen now? What was Stephanie doing there in the first place? From the looks of her clothing, the black hoodie, black leggings, gloves, and the nearby ski mask; she came to hurt someone, but it all backfired. Monica was the one to thank for that.

They would later find out that Stephanie planned to kill Keisha and kidnap the baby. The police found a car seat in the back of the car. Stephanie had no children. They also found a diary with the details of her plan covering several pages. There was a bag of baby clothes, pampers, blankets, and a few other items in the trunk just purchased at Target the day before. She was trying to hurt Darius in a way that she knew would be effective. She wanted to ruin his life. If she wasn't happy, neither would he be. She knew that he loved Keisha and that hurting his wife and stealing their baby would destroy him. That would not be happening today, or any other day. It was finally over.

2 GODPARENT DUTY

"Auntie's coming!" Monica jumped out of bed and headed into the guest room of the new home she and Jamel had just moved into. Though, it was officially a guestroom; it was decorated just for Keyana, but happened to have a queen-sized bed and dresser along with the crib Jamel had bought her after the christening. If they ended up with a house filled with guests, anyone occupying that room would have to get used to the little girls' décor. They would only use it for overflow guests and agreed to use the other three guestrooms first.

Keyana had been with them for the two weeks since the incident at Keisha and Darius's place. Keisha was still in a coma, which meant Darius had been by her side since she was admitted to the hospital. So that everyone could take turns visiting with her, they were rotating caring for the baby with her grandparents. Jamel and Monica were her Godparents and although both sets of grandparents lived nearby, Monica took the lead on taking care of her. She'd always wanted kids of her own but knew that it would be a while before she and Jamel sealed their commitment by getting married, especially with everything that was going on.

"Babe, why don't you get back in bed. I'll get her," said Jamel.

Getting back into bed, she let Jamel be the godfather he'd signed up to be. She was exhausted and needed to get her rest.

"Come here, cupcake. Come to Uncle Jamel," he reached to grab the little angel whose arms were already extended toward him.

He had fallen in love with her since the first day he saw her beautiful smile and light brown eyes at the hospital. She looked just like Keisha and there wasn't anything that Jamel wouldn't do for her. She was not only his goddaughter, but she was also like a niece considering the dynamics of the relationship he had with Keisha, and how close he and Darius had become.

After changing her diaper and preparing her bottle, he headed back into the master suite where Monica was already fast asleep. Looking at her, he felt sadness. She had been through so much. He knew that her killing Stephanie was wearing on her, even though it was self-defense. She had tossed and turned in her sleep every night for the past two weeks.

Jamel softly sat down on the edge of the bed to finish feeding the baby, then he placed Keyana between them before lying back down. After closing his eyes, he felt the soft touch of tiny fingers on his eye lid.

"You're not going to let Uncle Jamel go back to sleep, are you?"

Keyana giggled and touched his eyes again. In exchange, he touched hers. She smiled and chuckled. For the next few minutes, the two played a game of touching each other's eyes and noses, exchanging smiles and laughter.

With Monica's back to the two of them, she smiled. She knew that Jamel would make a wonderful husband and father someday. Life had been wonderful since the two of them entered their committed relationship. She knew that the only thing that could improve what they had was becoming his wife and having a couple of kids. But, she wouldn't rush it. Monica had learned that doing things in God's time was the best route and she was so glad that they had decided not to engage in anything that even resembled sex after leaving St. Thomas. Though the temptation was great, they were disciplined and agreed to maintain separate quarters in the house when the temptation became more than they could handle. The only intimacy they shared was in the form of a hug, a kiss, or holding hands. Over all, the relationship was just like any other relationship only without the sex.

Jamel picked up Keyana and placed her on Monica's side. She began to laugh as she grasped a handful of her long box braids. Monica turned over and grabbed Keyana. Holding her high into the air, she laughed until the sound became hollow. She was having the time of her life playing with her Auntie and Uncle Jamel.

"Babe, we better get up and get ready. We have to drop her off at Keisha's parent's house before heading to the hospital," Jamel reminded her, taking Keyana into his arms so that Monica could get out of bed.

"Yes, babe. You're right. We better pick up some breakfast for Darius before heading over. You know how he feels about hospital food."

Since Keisha and Darius had been together, the food served during her stays in the hospital because of her history of Sickle Cell Disease had left a bad taste in his mouth; literally; and he refused to eat it. In fact, whenever Keisha went in; he didn't want her eating it either.

"We can grab him some chicken and waffles from the Fish Market and then head over. By the time we get out of here, they should be open. You know how much he likes that," said Jamel.

The four of them frequented the place every now and then to listen to the House Band while enjoying dinner.

"Sounds good, I'm going to jump in the shower while you two finish playing your game of fingers and toesies," she laughed. She kissed Keyana on the cheek and Jamel on the lips before heading into the bathroom.

"She thinks she's funny," Jamel said to Keyana.

She laughed again, revealing her dimples; something she'd inherited from Keisha.

Jamel couldn't believe how smart his Goddaughter was. She seemed to always respond on cue, like she knew what he was saying.

"I believe we have a baby genius on our hands," he said. "Or a comedian."

He went into the guestroom to pick out Keyana's clothes for the day. Deciding on the hot pink dress with yellow tulips on the front and matching hot pink sandals, he placed them on the bed. Putting Keyana in her play yard, he set up the ironing board and iron.

"Dadadadada," Keyana said with her hands extended toward him.

"No, not Dada. Uncle Jamel. Can you say Uncle Jamel?"

She laughed. Falling backward, she grabbed one of her toys and began playing as if she'd given up on the idea of being freed from the play yard.

"Babe! You want me to iron your clothes?" Jamel yelled in the direction of the bathroom.

"Yes, if you wouldn't mind. Can you grab my dark blue True Religion jeans from the bottom right drawer and my white T-shirt with the rhinestones outlining the American flag from the middle one?" she yelled.

Jamel did as he was told and began ironing Monica's clothes. Glancing over his shoulder, he smiled at Keyana. She was now sound asleep.

"So now you want to go to sleep?" he smiled.

Reaching for her blanket, he covered her chubby legs and removed her toys before heading back into the master suite.

"Where's Keyana?" Monica asked.

"She played herself out. I left her in the play yard so that we could finish getting ready before waking her."

Jamel leaned into Monica and kissed her on the forehead before heading into the bathroom to take his shower. He tried not to stay close for too long because he knew that the slightest touch of her would ignite feelings inside of him that he thought were under control. He was dating Monica with a purpose and wanted to make an honest woman out of her very soon. In fact, as soon as they made it through the ordeal with Keisha; he would be purchasing the ring. One thing's for certain, Jamel had class. He would make sure that his proposal, the ring, and everything else was something that people would be talking about for years. He knew he was in love with Monica and wanted to make sure that everyone else knew it too.

3 PLEASE COME BACK

Darius rested his head on the bed. Holding Keisha's hand, he began to pray.

"Lord, please bring her back. I love this woman in a way that I've never loved anyone. She means the world to me and I want to have so many years with her that I need you to please bring her back. Lord, when we took our vows; I meant every word. I'm so sorry that something I did in my past has led to this. Please forgive me for ever letting Stephanie into my life, and for my part in landing my beautiful wife in this predicament. I ask you to heal her in her physical body, Lord. Give her the strength to fight her way back to me and our beautiful daughter. We both need her so much," Darius wiped the tears that were now falling down his cheeks before saying Amen.

Monica and Jamel fell back to let him have his moment before entering the room.

"Hey, man. We brought you some breakfast. You need to eat something. If you want to head to the house to take a shower and change clothes after you eat, we'll be here for her," said Jamel.

"I don't want to leave her, but I probably should at least run home and shower. How's my little angel doing?" Darius asked as he hugged Monica. "She's great. She hasn't been giving us any trouble at all. In fact, she's a joy to be around. I didn't realize that she laughed so much," Monica admitted.

"Yes, she's growing up so quickly. She's a happy baby. Was she happy to see Mom and Dad?"

"You know she was. They were about to sit down to breakfast and even though she already ate, she wanted some of what they had," said Monica. "That baby loves to eat!"

"She gets that from her daddy," admitted Darius.

"Well, how's my girl doing this morning?"

"She's still holding on, but I need her to come back. I miss holding her, talking to her; I just miss everything about her," Darius held his breath to keep the tears from falling again.

"It's going to be okay. Keisha is so strong. She'll make it through this and things will be better than before," said Monica, holding Darius's hand in hers.

As they sat in the chairs that aligned the side of Keisha's bed, Monica set up the blue tooth speaker she'd bought at Best Buy so that Keisha could listen to some of her favorite music. She had compiled some gospel songs along with some mild jazz and R & B into a playlist. Keisha loved music so much that they all believed it would be good for her. Darius wanted to believe that she could hear everything that was going on around her. So, music, prayer, and positive conversation could only help the situation.

While the friends sat around engaging in small conversations, Keisha's medical team entered the room.

"Good morning, Mr. Kingston. We're just making our rounds. I was reviewing Keisha's recent tests and her MRI revealed that she's in much better shape than we thought. The problem is in her labs. It appears that the trauma sent Keisha into a Sickle Cell Crisis, so we're working on that now. We're running the medication through her IV and monitoring the situation," said Dr. Mazzini without offering an overabundance of hope.

"Is she going to be okay, doctor?" Darius asked.

"We're doing our best," he said.

He didn't offer much other than that, but Darius and his family put their faith in a much higher power. Keisha would be okay.

Dr. Mazzini moved closer to Keisha's bedside and began looking at the monitor to review some of her vital signs. He made notes on the papers attached to the clipboard that he placed at the end of Keisha's bed.

"Someone will be around later this evening when we change shifts. If you need anything, please don't hesitate to let one of the nurses know. I'll be in the hospital for most of the day," he offered.

Darius walked into the hallway with Dr. Mazzini and the three young medical professionals that remained close by his side.

"Dr. Mazzini, do you think we could arrange for our baby to come up? I believe it might help the situation if Keisha knows she's here," Darius asked.

"I'm sure a short visit wouldn't hurt anything. It's been done before," he admitted. "We'll arrange for a visit tomorrow if that will work for you."

"Yes, doctor. That's perfect. Thank you so much. I'm sure the sound of our daughter will be good for her."

Darius returned to the room to let Monica and Jamel know that Keyana would be allowed to visit tomorrow.

"That's great! I'm sure Keyana misses her although she doesn't understand her absence," said Monica. "We can bring her by first thing in the morning. Just let us know what time."

Darius's mom and dad entered the room just as the three of them finished their conversation about Keyana's visit.

"Hi son," Candace grabbed Darius and gave him a hug. John did the same.

"How's my daughter-in-law doing this morning?" Candace headed to Keisha's side and gently rubbed her hair.

"She's hanging in there, Mom," Darius said.

"Monica, how are you doing? Are you hanging in there?"

Candace asked before giving Monica a hug too.

"Yes, I suppose I'm doing okay considering everything that's happened", said Monica.

Candace and Monica had spoken a few times about the incident that ended Stephanie's life, but saved her daughter-in-law's. She couldn't thank her enough for being the type of friend who would put her own life in jeopardy to save someone else. Though she didn't want to make mention of the incident in front of Keisha, the eye contact between the two said enough. Candace and John would forever be indebted to Monica for what she did. While everyone recognized that a young woman lost her life that day, she came there to kill Keisha, and no one could dismiss the facts that surrounded her visit to their home. No one in the family and not even the law.

"We'd better go. I told Sarah we would pick up Keyana so that they could head over here. Besides, I need to hold my grandbaby," she said.

"Darius, son. Please call us if anything changes," said John. He was the more reserved of his parents and even though he didn't talk much, Darius knew his heart was also breaking because of what the family was going through.

"Thanks, Dad," Darius said as he walked his parents to the elevator.

"Man, this is nuts!" said Jamel. "I still can't believe this is happening."

Jamel leaned toward Keisha and kissed her on her cheek. Holding her hand, he too said a prayer; although his was a silent one. He had so much that he wanted to say to God, so much he wanted Keisha to know. He truly believed he would get his chance to talk to her about his plans to marry Monica as soon as she was well. He was counting on it.

Monica looked at Jamel. Her heart became heavy as she realized that her dearest friend was struggling for her life, but the love of her life was also hurting because the woman he'd known for so many years; the one he called his little sister was lying there unable to speak, unable to move, unable to do anything at all. Jamel's love for Keisha was special. So, the fact that she was in this position didn't feel good to him. It didn't feel good to any one of them.

"Come back, baby girl. Come on back," he said.

Monica took her rightful place next to Jamel as the two of them sat quietly, watching their friend rest in what they prayed was a peaceful sleep.

Jamel smiled as he reminisced back to the day he met Keisha. They were on campus preparing for a Greek event. His fraternity and her sorority were hosting a mixer on campus and they were both in charge of promoting it, so they were handing out flyers and postcards to anyone they encountered. As he turned around to address a group of young ladies behind him, there she was. She was the most beautiful creature he had ever laid eyes on. He'd seen her around campus before and had even attended some events where she was also present, but they had never officially been introduced.

"We're promoting the same event," she smiled and handed the flyer back to him.

Considering they were both neophytes in their respective organizations, they were amongst the group who got out there to do whatever their big sisters and big brothers told them to do. Today, they were in charge of handing out flyers.

"I'm assuming you'll be there?" he asked.

"You know it," she said as she casually passed him by to continue the work that she was sent to do.

Watching her and her entourage of Sorors walk away, he just smiled and shook his head. Two days later at the actual event, he would meet Monica. Though admittedly, Jamel was overwhelmed by Keisha's beauty; he never approached her in any other way than as a friend. Over time, the two of them became inseparable. Monica would sometimes be a part of the things they did together and sometimes she would not. During those days, she was so busy chasing football players and the frat brothers who knew they had no good intentions for her. Yes, some of his frat brothers gave the organization a bad name. Jamel was just glad that he wasn't one of them. His parents had raised him to respect women. It was one of the life lessons that he was grateful for. One that he knew would make him a great husband someday.

"Babe, are you okay?"

The sound of Monica's voice snapped Jamel back to his current reality.

"Yes, I was just thinking about when we were in college, that's all," he admitted.

Monica knew how Jamel felt about Keisha. She knew he loved her dearly, but she never knew how deep his love for her truly went. It didn't matter now anyway. They were both with the partners they were supposed to be with. One day, the two of them would be happy just like Keisha and Darius; but with less drama than the two of them had endured in the short time they'd been married. Jamel wasn't about all of that. He was one who hated drama and tried to stay away from it at all cost. It wasn't worth it to him. He had too much going for him to let things like scandalous relationships get in his way. That was one thing that Monica would never have to worry about with him. There was no threat of his past catching up with him because he didn't live like that. Jamel was a good man. He was a better man than Darius when it came to matters of the heart, especially. Had he been the one going through a breakup with his lady, he would never have fallen victim to prey like Stephanie. It would have never happened because it wasn't in his nature. Jamel didn't think he was better than Darius. They were just cut from two different pieces of cloth.

4 A TIME TO REST

Darius popped his chicken and waffle platter into the microwave for a few seconds before removing it. He hadn't eaten in about 24 hours and knew that he needed to put something on his stomach. He had been so preoccupied with everything, that he wasn't taking care of himself. He had even lost a few pounds.

After devouring the plate of food, he headed to the bathroom to take a shower. While passing through the master suite, he couldn't help but visualize what had transpired there just a few weeks before.

"I let her down," he said aloud. "The one woman I would lay my entire life down for, I let her down."

Darius knew that the one-night stand that meant absolutely nothing to him was the cause for everything they were now going through. He never even cared about Stephanie. The truth is, he didn't even want to have sex with her that night but did it just because she was there, and the offer was on the table.

It was 10:00 P.M. when the doorbell rang. When he opened it, there was Stephanie standing there in a trench coat and black stilettos. She pushed her way around him and headed into his living room.

"What are you doing?" Darius asked as the trench coat hit the floor.

Stephanie stood in the middle of the room wearing nothing but pumps. Darius tried to resist, but his need for sexual pleasure took over and what happened Mwould set the stage for what he and his family were now going through.

Instantly, he began to feel faint as heat flooded his entire body. Why had he fallen to temptation that night? He knew that he was in love with Keisha and nothing else mattered, but in a few seconds, he'd attached himself to someone who would turn out to be unstable, obsessed, and psychotic. Now he was paying. He knew karma was real. Before meeting Keisha, Darius had broken many hearts because he didn't take relationships seriously. He had never found anyone he thought was worthy of such a commitment. That is until he met the woman he knew he would spend the rest of his life with. Now she was lying lifeless in a hospital bed struggling to hold on.

"Lord, please help me. Help Keisha. You know that she is the best thing that has ever happened to me. I found the one woman who could save me from myself. Please don't take her," he begged as tears poured down his face. Darius had never cried this much in his entire life.

He fell to his knees, "Father, Keyana and I need her so much. If you allow her to be okay, I promise you that I will never do anything to violate her trust ever again. My heart and soul belong to only one woman. Please, Lord."

After gathering his emotions, he turned on the shower and stepped inside. With his mind moving in several directions, he knew he would have to hire contractors to demolish the bedroom and rebuild it. Either that, or they would have to sell the house and buy another one. He didn't want to have the constant memory of what happened, of another woman in the bedroom that he shared with his wife; even if she had trespassed to gain access. The whole thing seemed so twisted, and because he knew how he felt about the situation; he could only imagine how Keisha might feel about it.

Darius lathered the soap in his washcloth and washed his body quickly so that he could take a power nap before heading back to the hospital. Falling across the bed wrapped in nothing but a towel, he was asleep just moments after his head hit the pillow.

"You need to get out of here," he said in his sleep.

Darius jumped. Looking around the room, he realized he was having a nightmare. The house would have to go. He needed it sold like yesterday. He would plan to have some of their things moved back to Keisha's house until they could figure out what to do next.

"Thank God, we didn't sell it."

The two of them had finally agreed on renting out Keisha's place and not selling it. The original renters had opted for a six-month lease because they were waiting for their house to be completed. So, they hadn't found another renter. This would work out perfectly, at least for now. Though, he hated uprooting Keyana from her nursery; he would just have to paint and decorate her other room to make her comfortable until they either built or found another house. He just needed his family to feel safe in their surroundings. He didn't want Keisha having nightmares or flashbacks about what happened, and he knew if he was having them she probably would too.

"I miss my babies. The big one and the little one," he admitted.

He grabbed the vibrating cell phone from the nightstand.

"Hello?"

"Hey, Darius; you need to get up here quick!"

"Jamel, I'm on my way. What's going on?" he said while trying to put on his sweats without dropping the phone. "Is Keisha okay? What's going on?"

"Man, you're not going to believe this. Monica was holding Keisha's hand and she squeezed it," Jamel's voice shook as he described to Darius how it happened. "It wasn't a tight squeeze, but she did it. I actually saw her fingers move."

After lacing up his Nike's, Darius jumped into his Range

Rover and sped out of the driveway.

"Jamel, I'll be there in fifteen minutes. Thank God! My baby's gonna be okay,"

"Yeah, man. The doctors are with her now. Monica's still in the room talking to her. I'm not sure if she's able to respond or anything yet, though."

"If she moved her hand, she's coming around," Darius said confidently.

"I'll be there in a few minutes. I need to call our parents to let them know. I think they need to get up there with Keyana," he said.

"Okay, man. See you in a few minutes."

Darius pressed his parents' number from the recent calls on the display in the car.

"Hello?" said Candace.

"Mom, can you and dad meet me at the hospital with Keyana?"

"Of course, what's wrong?"

"Nothing's wrong. Keisha just moved her fingers. She squeezed Monica's hand. I think we all need to be there when she comes around. I believe this is it."

"John? Grab Keyana. We have to get to the hospital."

"Oh, thank God!" Darius could hear his father's voice in the background. He did what he was told.

"I'm on my way back there now. I'll see you when you get there, okay?" I need to call Sarah and Marcus."

"Darius, you just focus on getting there safely. I'll call them," Candace said. "We're on our way."

5 SIGNS OF IMPROVEMENT

Darius spotted Candace and John walking toward the hospital entrance with Keyana in her stroller.

"Mom!" Darius called out.

They both stopped to wait for him to catch up.

"Hi Son," Candace grabbed his neck to give him a hug.

"Dadadada," Keyana stretched out her hands toward her father.

"Hey, Angel. Daddy has missed you," he said, after removing her from the stroller, he gave her a kiss in the crease of her neck.

Keyana began to laugh. She was looking more and more like Keisha every day.

"You okay, man?" John asked his son.

"Yeah, Pops. I'm hanging in there. Just missing my family."

"It's going to be fine, son. Just keep praying, keep the faith, and trust God," he said. "I know you're probably tired of hearing things like that, but it's the truth and it works."

"No, Pops. I definitely believe in the power of prayer. You and Mom raised me, remember? It's all I knew growing up. I just wished I hadn't strayed from what you and Mom were trying to do."

"You know you can fix that, don't you? It's never too late to get your life right as long as you're still breathing. You and Keisha have been living your lives the right way since you got married, so please don't beat yourself up about this. Stephanie was obviously crazy, and if it hadn't been you; it would have been some other guy."

"I guess you're right. I just should have kept it moving when I met her, and we wouldn't be here right now dealing with all of this. Keisha wouldn't be in a coma. Keyana would have her mother home and I would have my wife. Man, this is crazy. I still can't believe it happened, but I'm praying it's about to end, and I will never get myself caught up in anything like this again. I just want to get this in our past and leave it there. I pray we all can."

The three of them walked in silence for the rest of the trip to the ICU. Keyana had fallen asleep and was snuggling her stuffed bumble bee tightly. Darius placed her back into the stroller.

"Keisha? Can you hear me?" asked Dr. Mazzini.

He shined a light into Keisha's eyes that were now open, though she wasn't responding to his questions.

Darius rushed to Keisha's side when he realized that her eyes were not only open, but she was blinking.

"Dada," said Keyana as her sleep was disturbed by the hospital room commotion.

Darius grabbed Keyana out of her stroller and carried her closer to Keisha. She placed her head softly on her father's shoulder as she looked at her mother lying in the hospital bed. Though, she was too young to understand what was going on, she obviously recognized her.

Suddenly, Keisha's eyes filled with tears. Her inability to speak didn't matter at that moment because there was at least another sign that she recognized everyone and was eventually going to be okay. Sarah and Marcus entered the room just as Darius placed Keyana on the bed next to her mother. She gently laid her head on her mother's stomach and rested there.

Keisha's fingers began to move.

"She's moving her hands again," said Monica.

Dr. Mazzini held her hand. "Keisha, can you squeeze my hand for me?"

Doing as she was told, she squeezed it. More tears fell from her eyes.

Sarah rushed to the other side of Keisha's bed.

"Keisha, it's Mom." Sarah grabbed her hand and held it tightly.

Keisha's eyes followed her mother's voice. Tears continued to stream steadily down her cheeks. Her left arm moved slightly toward Keyana. She wanted to touch her daughter, but just couldn't get there yet.

"It's okay, honey. We're all here. It's okay," said Marcus who was now standing at Sarah's side with is arm around her waist.

"Keisha, come on baby," said Darius. "Keyana and I really need you."

Her eyes moved to the other side of the bed, in the direction of Darius's voice. Keisha nervously looked from one side of the room to the other as if she had no idea what was going on around her but recognized the room full of people who all loved and adored her. Everyone sat around the hospital room while Dr. Mazzini examined and assessed Keisha's condition. He and the nurse removed the tubes from her nose and her mouth, then they all just waited.

"Her throat is probably very sore right now because of the tube, but I feel confident that she will be able to speak as soon as she's ready," he said. "We're going to need to run some labs to get a look at what's going with her blood right now, but it seems that she may even be on the other side of the Sickle Cell Crisis too. Anyway, the labs will confirm this. Darius, you have a very strong and determined wife."

"Yes, Dr., I realize that. It's part of the reason I married her."

"Well, we'll need to keep her here in the ICU for at least one more night to observe her very closely. After that, I believe it will be safe to move her to another room," admitted the doctor. "Based on how she feels, we'll need to get her up and moving in the next couple days to ensure she's stable on her feet before even considering letting her go. She may need a little rehab. I'm not sure yet, but she's headed in the right direction."

"This is by far the best news I've heard since this all began. Thank you, Dr. Mazzini."

Keyana rested on her mother's chest until she fell asleep. Seeing the two of them together made Darius's heart warm. He couldn't wait to get her home where he could take care of her himself. For now, he would let the doctors at MedStar Southern Maryland Hospital do what they had to do to get her to a stable place.

Keisha's eyes wandered the room from one face to the next before closing her eyes to rest. There was something very peaceful about seeing her there with Keyana. The love between the two of them was obvious. Thank God Stephanie's attempt to sever it had failed. Keisha was strong. She could not be broken.

6 I LOVE YOU MORE THAN LOVE

After everyone had gone their separate ways for the evening, Darius rested next to Keisha's bedside taking in the hospital noise that was going on around him. Opening his eyes, he observed Keisha looking at him.

"Hey love, how are you feeling?" he asked.

Darius realized that the chance of receiving a response was at 50 percent. He just held her hand, not expecting too much but happy that she was now conscious and alert.

"I love you more than love," Keisha squeezed his hand.

Darius sat up in the chair. He pressed the nurse's call button to summon someone to the room.

"I love you too, baby! More than love!" he said.

"Is everything okay, Mr. Kingston?" asked the middle-aged nurse who'd just entered the room.

"She just spoke," he said through laughter.

"Could you make out what she said?" asked Nurse Shannon.

"She said, I love you more than love," he admitted.

"Okay, she's not making much sense, I guess but at least she's talking," said Nurse Shannon.

"No, you don't understand. She's making perfect sense. It's something I say to her all the time. I love you more than love. She knows exactly what she said," Darius insisted.

"Oh, wow! I'll page the doctor," said Nurse Shannon, but before leaving the room, she checked Keisha's blood pressure and pulse.

"Keisha? Mrs. Kingston, how are you?" she asked.

"I'm fine," Keisha said. This time, her voice was slightly above a whisper.

"See? I told you," said Darius.

Nurse Shannon offered him a huge smile, "yes you did."

"Where's Keyana?" she asked Darius.

"She's with your parents. I'm getting ready to call them now," he said waiting patiently for Nurse Shannon to finish what she was doing. He wanted to hug his wife, to kiss her lips.

"Keisha, do you need anything?" she asked.

"I could use some water or apple juice. I'm hungry too," she said.

"Oh yes, she's back," said Darius. "My baby's back."

"I'll get you some juice, water, and how about some warm broth to start? We want to make sure that you can keep it down. You haven't eaten in a while, so we want to take this slow, okay? Once the doctor comes in, I'll see about getting you something else."

"Okay."

Nurse Shannon exited the room. Darius sat on the edge of the bed and held Keisha in his arms.

"Babe, I'm so glad you're okay. I'm so sorry that this happened. I know it's all my fault, and I'm so sorry," he admitted.

"It's okay, Darius. Based on her actions over the past year or so, it was bound to happen sooner or later. We just have to make sure that she gets a lot of time for what she did, or at least some psychiatric help."

Darius looked at Keisha, realizing that she had no idea how it had all ended. He would choose a more appropriate time to tell her.

Darius called Sarah and Marcus before calling his parents, Monica and Jamel, then Shawn, Pam, and Cynthia. Finally, he called Tonya at the bank, so she could inform the team that Keisha was okay. She was still on a leave of absence from work, and now she might never go back, and Darius was okay with it. He could more than afford to support the family. Besides, Keisha had other talents. If she wanted to just do makeovers, that was okay with him. She could turn it into a full-fledged business if she wanted to. She was just that good at it. If she chose to just take care of Keyana, that was okay too. After all of this, Darius felt safer knowing that she was at home taking it easy and not stressing herself out over anything that could cause her to go into crisis. He would make sure that he wasn't responsible for anything bad like this ever again.

Darius sat back on the side of the bed and began stroking Keisha's hair.

"We just need to get you back to 100 percent, so I can take you home. We need you there," he said.

"I miss being there. I miss our bed, our home, everything," she admitted.

"Keisha, I was thinking that you might want us to move back to your house for a while," Darius said.

"No, I don't want to do that. We have a home together and that's where I want to go," she insisted.

"Babe, are you sure? It hasn't even been that easy for me to sleep there. If you want to go back to the other house, I support that. I was even thinking we might want to consider selling the house and buying a new one."

"Yes, we should probably sell it; but until we do it's our home," she said.

"Well, you're the queen of the castle so if that's what you want; that's what it is," Darius admitted.

He kissed Keisha softly on her lips and held her hand in his. He knew that she was so strong-willed that there was no chance he was going to win. Besides, it was about what made her happy, and that was it. If Keisha said they were going to stay in the house on Hickory Street, that's where they were going to stay. They both loved that house and had made so many happy memories there despite the tragedy that unfolded. Hopefully one day, Darius would be able to put it out of his mind. For now, it didn't seem that Keisha was having that much of a problem doing it. That's all that mattered. He made a mental note to call a contractor to make some changes to the room. A fresh coat of paint, new carpet, and a closet expansion would probably work; at least for now. He would also rearrange the furniture to give the room a different look. If she insisted on staying there, these small changes might be good for a while. It might even help him to put the thoughts out of his mind. What really mattered was having his family at home where they belonged. No psycho stalker could come between that.

Sarah and Marcus were the first to arrive at the hospital after receiving Darius's call. Sarah was anxious to see Keisha. She would know how she was truly doing once she was able to talk to her. A mother just knows some things because of the bond shared with her daughter.

"How's my beautiful daughter doing this morning?"

"Hi Mom, Dad. I'm doing okay," Keisha said. "I'm ready to go home, though."

"I'm sure you are. Hopefully soon, Dr. Mazzini will agree to that."

"I just want to rock Keyana in our favorite rocking chair," she admitted. "I've missed her so much. Her and Darius both."

"I know you have, Sweetie. This will all be over soon. Then you can pick up the pieces to your life and leave this all in the past. At least you don't have to worry about Stephanie ever bothering you or your family ever again."

"Yes, I agree," said Keisha.

"Mom, can I speak to you for a second?" Darius asked while heading toward the door.

"Sure Darius, is everything okay?" she asked.

"Mom, Keisha doesn't know that Stephanie is dead. I didn't want to tell her while she was still in a somewhat fragile condition," he whispered as they left the room.

"Oh, I see. Well, you're going to have to tell her soon. At least the news isn't talking about it anymore. You might want to notify the others before they get here. Someone is bound to slip up and mention something otherwise."

"I'll send them all a text message right now."

"Okay. In the meantime, we better get back in there. I'll mention it to Marcus."

"Darius, is everything okay?" Keisha asked as they re-entered the room.

"Yes, Babe. Everything is fine. Monica and Jamel are on their way with Keyana."

Keisha's face lit up at the mention of her daughter's name. She adored her and was actually thinking about having another baby within the next couple of years. Though, she hadn't mentioned it to Darius yet.

Dr. Mazzini walked into the room followed by Pam and Shawn. "Mrs. Kingston, I'm arranging to have you moved to a private room very shortly. You're progressing very well, and we believe now is a good time to start getting you ready for your transition home. After we're certain that you can handle solid foods and are able to walk on your own, you should be on your way. That process could take anywhere from a few days to a couple of weeks. It depends on how up to it you are," he admitted. "I spoke to Dr. Cavanaugh earlier today. She'll be over here to check on you sometime this evening," he continued.

"Thanks, Dr. Mazzini," Keisha said.

Keisha wasn't aware, but Dr. Cavanaugh had visited with her a few times a week since she was admitted.

"That's great news, doctor," said Marcus. "We're definitely looking forward to taking her home as soon as she's ready."

"Yes, doctor. I'm really ready to get back to my life," Keisha said.

Darius looked at Keisha to determine from her expression if she was truly ready to go back there. There were no signs that indicated anything different. She was handling it very well. He prayed she didn't wake up one day and realize the trauma she'd really been through. He didn't know what that might do to her and he didn't want to find out. Keisha had been through a very stressful and traumatic event that could have caused someone weak to fall apart. She was stronger than he knew. But again, she was a fighter. A survivor for sure.

7 WELCOME HOME

The banner hanging across the front of the porch was waving in the wind when Darius pulled the Range Rover into the driveway and into the garage. Keisha smiled as she realized she was finally home. Sarah opened the door leading into the kitchen holding Keyana in her arms. It was hard to believe it had been more than a month since she'd been there.

Darius ran to the passenger side door to help his wife out of the car. Keyana giggled and bounced in her grandmother's arms. It was as if she knew her mother was finally home to stay. She had been so good through the whole ordeal that everyone enjoyed spending time with her.

Darius helped Keisha up the three steps leading into the house. She was moving at a normal pace, but very cautiously. Candace took Keyana from Sarah so that she could hug her daughter.

"Welcome home, Sweetie," she said. "I'm so glad you're finally here."

"Thanks, Mom. Yes, I'm happy to finally be home."

"Come here, Babe," Darius said while guiding Keisha to her favorite family room recliner.

After getting her comfortably seated, he reclined the chair and placed a blanket over her legs. The room was filled with all their friends and even some of the neighbors from across the street and next door.

Ed and Lisa had moved in next door to Darius and Keisha in the middle of all of Stephanie's drama. In fact, Ed had called 911 at least three times to report a stranger lurking around the house late at night. Little did he know that the family was being stalked and it would result in one dead and one seriously injured.

"Keisha, it's so good to have you back. Keyana and Tasha can pick up with their play dates as soon as you're up to it. If you need some time to yourself, I'd be happy to take her to some of the activities when we go. Just let me know," said Lisa.

"Thanks, Lisa. I really appreciate it," said Keisha, knowing she had no intentions of letting Keyana out of her sight, at least for a while.

"Well, we're not going to stay. We know you need your rest. I baked a lasagna for you. Your Mom is warming it up right now. I hope you enjoy it. Ed made a huge salad too. We thought it might help considering. It'll keep anyone from having to cook. At least for tonight," she offered.

"Lisa, thank you guys so much! You can't even imagine how thankful I am."

Keisha leaned forward to hug Lisa before she and her husband headed toward the front door. Over the next hour, Thomas and Angela from across the street dropped off a homemade cake and banana pudding, and a seafood casserole. Angela was one of Keisha's employees. They had gone to closing on their home while Keisha was in the hospital.

"Keisha, we're so glad you're okay. The guys at work wanted me to tell you that they all miss you. Those flowers over there on the island are from everyone," said Angela. "We're going to get out of your hair. Please let me know if you need anything. You know where to find me."

"Thanks, Angela. Congratulations on the new house, too," Keisha said. "I'll have to get over there soon to check it out. I never knew the previous neighbors, so this will be my first time in there. I'm so proud of you, girl!"

"Thank you," Angela said with a smile on her face. She always looked up to Keisha and getting acceptance from her meant so much.

Soon, the house was just filled with the old gang. Pam, Shawn, and Cynthia had cleaned the entire house from top to bottom in anticipation of Keisha coming home. She rested in the recliner with Keyana draped across her chest fast asleep. Holding her baby was all she wanted to do. Running her hand through her soft curly hair made her smile. Things were starting to feel like normal again.

By 7:00 o'clock, everyone had gone. Keisha was ready to call it a night.

"Babe, let me help you up the stairs," said Darius.

Draping his arm around Keisha's waist, he helped her up to the bedroom.

"Darius, what did you do?" she asked. "The room looks amazing!"

"Thanks, Babe. I had some work done for you. I figured since you didn't want to move, the least I could do was make it look different than it did before you left," Darius admitted. The room really did look good.

"Would you mind running a bath for me?" she asked.

"Sure babe. Anything for you."

Keisha rested on the bed while Darius prepared her bath. She admired what her husband had done to the room. The walls were painted in a beautiful khaki color with new paintings, new furniture, and carpeting. Keisha knew he had done it to make her more comfortable about being back in there, and she loved him for it.

Darius helped Keisha to the bathroom where he removed her clothes before placing her gently in the warm sudsy water. Then he removed his clothes and climbed in. Darius squeezed body wash on the new bath sponge he'd bought for her before rubbing it gently across her shoulders.

"Babe, you don't have to do that," she said.

"I want to."

"Darius, you did an amazing job in the bedroom. The bathroom too. How did you manage to get all this done in such a short time span?" she asked.

"I hired the best contractors that money could buy," he admitted. "I also let Monica and Pam pick out the furniture. You've known them so long, I knew they were bound to nail it on the first try and they did."

"Yes, they did!"

"Jamel's firm actually did the architectural design," Darius admitted while looking around the room to admire the work.

"This looks like something Jamel would have designed. I'll have to thank him soon."

"Wait until you see what he did with your closet. You know the sixth bedroom that was on the other side of your closet and this bathroom?"

"Yes."

"Well, it's gone. We now only have five bedrooms, but there's still the one in the basement that we're using as an office. I hope you don't mind."

"Babe! That was a huge room!"

"Well, now you have a huge dressing room and closet. I can't wait for you to see it."

"Neither can I," she smiled.

Keisha relaxed in the bubble bath with her back on Darius's chest until the water began to get cold.

"We'd better get out of here. My hands are shriveling."

Darius helped her out of the tub and dried her body with the towel. He missed her so very much. Just looking at her standing there began to excite him, but he didn't know if she was ready, so he thought of something else. Keisha exited the bathroom's double doors and headed toward her dresser to retrieve a pair of panties and Victoria's Secret nightshirt. Darius watched her get dressed. She was so beautiful. After dressing, she headed to Darius's chest of drawers and pulled out a pair of boxers. She handed them to him.

"What about my pajamas?"

"What pajamas? That's all you need," she teased.

Saying nothing else, he put them on.

Keisha checked the video monitor on the nightstand to make sure that Keyana was okay. Then she headed down the hall and into her nursery. She was sound asleep. Kissing her chubby cheek, Keisha headed back to the master suite.

"Now, let's check out this closet you've been bragging about," she said.

Darius grabbed her hand and guided her through the closet, which now had a new entryway and a hallway that wasn't there before. The room was the size of their master suite. There were shoe inlets lining either side of one portion of the room. All of Keisha's shoes were carefully displayed. There was another wall with cubby holes especially for her designer handbags. In the center of the room was an island with drawers on all four sides. Then toward the back of the room was a separate section that contained upper and lower level hanging racks where all of Keisha's clothes were displayed. Finally, Darius had purchased a beautiful chaise lounge that sat in the center of the room. There was a mirrored wall where Keisha could admire herself each day after getting dressed. There were three windows so that natural sunlight could get in. Jamel had also had the contractors install skylights across the ceiling. It was a woman's dream closet.

"Oh my God, babe! This is absolutely amazing!"

"I'm glad you like it."

"Come here, you," she said," draping her arms around his neck and placing her lips gently on his. "I love you so much. Thank you for all of this."

"Anything for you, love. You know that."

Darius picked his wife up in his arms, carried her back into the bedroom and placed her gently on the bed.

"You need anything?" he asked.

"No, just you."

Darius quickly climbed into bed to hide his arousal from Keisha.

"Babe, don't start nothing that you know you're not

supposed to be doing."

"What do you mean? The doctor said I could resume regular activities as soon as I felt up to it."

"He wasn't talking about sex, though."

"Yes, he was. Sex was on the list."

"What list?"

"The one in my bag that we haven't unpacked yet."

Darius jumped out of bed to get the discharge papers from Keisha's bag. Scanning through the list of dos and don'ts, and there it was. A message that indicated Keisha could resume sexual activity as soon as she was ready.

"Alrighty then," Darius said to himself before climbing back into bed.

Yes, he wanted it; but he wouldn't push the issue. If she made the first move, he would surely oblige; but if not, he would just go to sleep. He held his wife in a spooning position, kissed her neck and closed his eyes. Within fifteen minutes, they were both asleep.

8 IT'S 2:00 A.M.

Keisha awoke to movement in the room. There was Darius looking out the window into the backyard. After the incident with Stephanie, he'd had cameras installed on the front porch, back deck, and leading down to the basement door. ADT had also installed a very sophisticated alarm system. There was no way that anyone would ever get into the house again who was not invited.

"Babe, what are you doing? It's 2:00 A.M!" she asked.

"I was just checking the alarm and the cameras again. Plus, I wanted to check on Keyana."

"Don't let me find out that you're paranoid now, and you know Keyana's been sleeping through the night since she was four weeks old. That girl sleeps like a rock. Come back to bed."

"I know, but I changed her diaper."

"Did she wake up?"

"No."

"See? I told you," Keisha laughed.

Darius knew she was right. Keyana slept very soundly while Keisha was a light sleeper. The slightest movement or sound would wake her up. The video monitor was on the nightstand on Keisha's side of the bed, so she always heard her first. He returned to the bed and cradled his wife in his arms.

"I love you so much," he said.

"I love you too, babe. More than you could ever imagine."

"More than love?"

"You know it."

Keisha gently kissed Darius's lips. She reached into his boxers and released him. It had been over a month since they had been intimate. She knew that if he missed her as much as she missed him, he must be ready to explode. They had never gone for more than a day without making love unless she was sick.

Lifting her nightshirt over her head, he kissed each of her nipples before resting his head on her breasts. He didn't want to hurt her, so he was hesitant.

"Babe, what's wrong? The doctor said I was good to go, so let's go," she said.

"What? Who is this woman?" he laughed. "You're a little pushy, I see."

"No, I've just been missing my husband."

"I see," Darius said as he felt the moisture that had settled in her panties. He slid them down to her ankles before throwing them on the floor.

Darius entered Keisha's body. Moving in slow but steady strokes, he thought back to the last time they made love.

"Babe, I've missed you so much," he admitted.

"Don't talk," she insisted.

The two lovers engaged in a regular round of lovemaking without saying a word. There were just gazes from one to the other. Darius picked her up and carried her to the dresser where he placed her gently on the edge.

"Oh, baby," she said, wrapping her legs around his waist.

The strokes became harder and steadier, but he tried to control himself.

When they were both satisfied, he carried her back to the bed and kissed her stomach. With her legs still wrapped around his waist, she held him there. They held each other for several minutes before climbing back under the sheets that were now cold again. It was the first time they'd made love in a while, but it would set the stage for many more nights of hot, steamy sex between two lovers who were so emotionally and physically connected. Keisha had a thing for waking up in the middle of the night to make love. This 2:00 A.M. session was no different.

9 THE TRUTH ABOUT STEPHANIE

Darius stared out the bedroom window with Keyana in his arms. Keisha was still sound asleep. Since coming home from the hospital, he noticed she was a little late to rise each morning. He supposed it was because she didn't have to get up at 5:00 A.M. to prepare for work. So, the sun usually rose before she did. It was now 8:30 and Darius and Keyana had already had breakfast, taken a bath, and were dressed.

"What are you two doing?"

"Just watching a rabbit running around the backyard. How are you feeling this morning?"

"I feel fine. I can't believe I slept so late. I wanted to get up at 7:00, but it looks like I missed it."

"Why did you need to get up so early?"

"To put a load of laundry into the washer."

"Keisha, really? You're just coming home from the hospital and you're worried about laundry? I guess you haven't been in the laundry room because Monica already did it. She washed everything."

"I had everything under control while you were gone. Besides, we've got a great bunch of friends. They did so much to help so that I could spend as much time with you at the hospital as I could. Keyana stayed with Monica and Jamel most of the time."

"I'll have to think of something nice to do for them. They're the best, aren't they?"

"Yes, they sure are. They both love you very much."

"Yes, they do."

Darius placed Keyana and her stuffed bumble bee onto the bed. She placed its wing in her mouth like a mother transporting her baby pup and crawled in Keisha's direction. She rested her head on her stomach as if her journey across the mattress had been long and strenuous. Keisha smiled and rubbed the light brown curls that framed her daughter's face.

"Babe. I want to talk to you about something."

"Okay, what's up?"

"I was wondering if you wanted to talk about the day that Stephanie got into the house."

"Okay."

"Well, what do you remember about that day?"

Keisha stared off into the distance as she recalled the incident.

"I remember the doorbell ringing just as I was putting Keyana down for her late morning nap," she hesitated. "When I came downstairs and looked outside I didn't see anyone. So, I went into the kitchen to get a cup of coffee. Monica was supposed to be on her way over, so initially I thought it was her. Then, I heard the doorbell again. I headed back toward the door, but this time I could see that there was someone standing there," she hesitated again. "When I opened the door, Stephanie pushed her way into the house. She was wearing black leggings, a black sweatshirt, black Nikes, and a black baseball cap."

Keisha's breathing became strained as she recalled the rest of the details.

"Babe, are you sure you want to continue?"

"Yes, I need to make sure you know everything. Anyway, she started yelling at me for stealing her man and said that I was going to pay. We both were. The next thing I remember is rolling around on the carpet trying to drag her out of the house, but she hit me with something and I fell backwards. When I fell, she made a mad dash for the stairs and before I knew it, she was headed in the direction of Keyana's nursery. The commotion had caused her to start crying, so Stephanie knew where she was."

"Then what?"

"I ran up the stairs and we struggled some more. I wasn't about to let her get anywhere near Keyana. She was screaming at the top of her lungs. I remember fighting with her until we were standing in here. Then she hit me again and I don't remember anything else. Maybe you could fill in the blanks."

Darius seized the moment to explain what happened to Stephanie. She was going to have to know one way or another and he felt it was best if the news came from him.

"Well, sometime after that Monica showed up. She rang the doorbell and knocked on the door a few times. Then she called both phones, but there was no answer. She became concerned, so she called Jamel who in turn called me. Before we could get here, Monica was already in the house. She found Keyana still crying in her crib. You were unconscious on the floor right over there," Darius pointed to the area of the floor near the window. "After calling 911, she realized that someone was hiding in your closet. That's where she found Stephanie."

"Wow! That's insane, isn't it?"

"Well, there's more. You sure you're ready for this?"

"Babe, I told you I wanted to know, so please."

Darius took a deep breath before continuing, "Okay, the two of them struggled and Monica ended up shooting her in self-defense."

"I thought she was in jail. Is she in the hospital? Was she in the same hospital where I was?"

"Babe."

"What, Darius? What is going on?"

Stephanie's dead. She died almost instantly."

Tears filled Keisha's eyes as allowed the impact of Darius's words to set in. She couldn't stand Stephanie, but she never wanted her dead. She was a sick woman and needed help.

"Darius, please. You're telling me that she died right here in our room?"

"In your closet. That's why I had the room renovated. I didn't want you to have the memory of it etched in your mind every time you came in here."

"The truth is, I don't remember anything that happened beyond what I've already told you. It's a bit creepy, but things look so different that I believe I'll be okay. We can give it a try for a while."

Suddenly, a look of terror appeared on Keisha's face.

"Oh my God! What about Monica? Did they charge her with anything?"

"No babe, it was determined that Monica acted in self-defense. The 911 dispatcher was on the line and heard the whole thing. After the detectives listened to the 911 call, they knew exactly what happened. There was no question about it."

"I need you to drive me to Monica and Jamel's place," Keisha demanded as she moved Keyana onto the mattress so that she could get out of bed.

"No, I'm not doing that. They'll be over at 12:30 for lunch."

"I can't believe Monica sacrificed herself to save us," Keisha wiped the tears from her cheeks. "Stephanie was trying to kill me."

"Yes, and she wanted to take Keyana after she got rid of you. Apparently, she was trying to hurt me in the worst possible way that she could. Without you and Keyana, my life means nothing."

"I know what you mean," Keisha picked up Keyana and kissed her forehead.

Walking over to Darius, she kissed him too.

"Thank God for Monica. Things could have gone so much differently had she not shown up when she did. Please tell me that Stephanie didn't do anything to Keyana."

"No, she was examined at the hospital and nothing was

found."

"Okay."

"Is that it? You're not going to yell? You're not going to ask me if it was all worth it?"

"Babe, we've all suffered enough. We need to figure out how we're going to put this behind us and never let anything like this happen ever again."

"Keisha, you already know. I told you how much I regretted even getting involved with her at all. I meant it."

"Do you think we need to go to counseling? Speaking of counseling, have you still been going to your AA meetings? With all this excitement, I hope you've been able to attend."

"Yes, babe. I've been going. To answer your initial question, I don't know if we need to go to counseling unless you feel that we should. I'll support that. I just need us to be okay."

The calmness of Keisha's voice said that she would be okay. She wasn't cold or distant toward Darius even though they were suffering from the consequences of his actions. She loved her husband and wouldn't let this come between them. After all, Darius was honest about his involvement with Stephanie from the beginning. It's not like he hid anything from her. So, she would take it like a real woman and would help him to move beyond it. They would be okay. The family unit was as strong as ever and nothing or no one would ever come between them again.

10 FRIENDS FOR LIFE

Monica and Jamel arrived at the Kingston residence promptly at 12:30. Darius had been in the kitchen for the past two hours preparing lunch. He'd picked up several two-pound lobsters and jumbo shrimp from the seafood market and was steaming them together in a pot with fresh corn on the cob and baby potatoes. He even grilled a couple of steaks with some fresh mushrooms, green peppers, and onions. Keisha looked at him putting the finishing touches on the lunch spread while Jamel pulled leftover banana pudding from the fridge.

"Darius told me what happened," Keisha reached for her friend's hand. "Thank you so much for making sure that Keyana and I were okay."

"Girl, you don't have to thank me for that. There was no way that I was going to let anything happen to either one of you. Trust and believe. I'm sorry it ended the way it did, but I did what I had to do. We were struggling over the gun when I shot her. It's over now, though."

"Are you going to be okay? That's a lot to carry around with you."

"I'm fine. Unfortunately, she got what was coming to her.

How are you going to plot to kill someone and take their child? I don't know a single person who wouldn't have reacted the same way I did. It was her or me. If she killed me, then you would have surely been killed too. God only knows where Keyana would be right now."

"Yeah, you're right."

"So, let's put it out of our minds and enjoy this delicious lunch your husband has prepared for us. Come on," reaching for Keisha's other hand, she helped her up from the sofa.

"You're right."

After Darius blessed the food, the couples engaged in great conversation and lunch without a single mention of Stephanie or the tragedy.

"So, Keisha; when do you think you'll be up for some travel?" Jamel asked.

"I don't know. I guess after I see the doctor for my follow up, I should be clear to get away. Why? What's up?"

"I was just thinking that we all need to get away. You know, just the five of us. I was thinking about someplace different. Someplace neither of us has ever been before."

"Okay, what do you have in mind?"

"What about Turks and Caicos?"

"Wow! Now that's a trip! What do you think, babe?" looking at Darius for acceptance.

"Yeah, that definitely sounds like a winner to me."

"Okay, when's your follow up?"

"It's actually on Wednesday. I'll talk to the doctor about it then."

"Okay, well one of you please call me after the appointment so that I can start booking the flights and make the resort reservations. This one's on me," said Jamel.

"We should be taking you on a trip after everything you've done for us over the past six weeks or so."

"No, you don't owe us anything. That's what friends do, remember? You would have done the same thing for us."

"Yeah, you're right. Turks and Caicos? Keisha, how do you feel about leaving Keyana with Mom and Dad for this trip?"

"I suppose that would be okay. She's probably going to think I abandoned her again, though. Jamel, how soon are you trying to go?"

"Next month."

"Oh yeah, she should be okay by then. That gives me a month to love on her real good before we go."

"Monica, have you heard from Cynthia?"

"She came by the hospital a couple of times while you were in there, but I haven't seen her that much. She's been decorating the new house and with the new government contract, I'm sure she's very busy," Monica paused to take a sip from her glass of lemonade. "You know, Rico wrote her a letter."

"What the? You mean he had the nerve to do something like that?"

"Sure did."

"He apologized for what he did to her and said he wanted her to visit him."

"Lord, please don't tell me she did it."

"She said she wasn't, but I don't know."

"That fool is just trying to get some money on his books," said Jamel.

Keisha looked at Jamel to determine if he was agitated by the conversation or not. After all, Rico had really hurt Monica too.

"Have you been by the branch lately?" Keisha changed the subject.

"Yes, I've been by there several times to transact business. The guys miss you so much."

"I don't know when I'll go back there, if at all."

Darius smiled. He didn't want her to go back, but he knew it had to be her decision. Banking had gotten to be a dangerous career these days and after everything she'd been through, he felt safer knowing she was not out there jeopardizing herself. He was okay with her staying at home if that's what she wanted but hadn't had the discussion yet. They had plenty of time to talk about it.

"Man, this lobster is delicious!" said Jamel. "Everything is, and I don't know what you put on this steak, but I can't stop eating it."

"I just threw a little of this and a little of that on it," Darius bragged. "I'm glad you're enjoying it."

After finishing their lunch, the friends sat around catching Keisha up on what had been going on in each of their lives. Monica brought Keyana down from her nursery so that they could watch her crawl around the carpet. She had just gotten good at it. They let the baby entertain them while the men cleared the table and washed the dishes. Keisha loved seeing the two of them together. They were the only two men that she'd ever loved besides her father, though the love she had for each of them was different.

"Man, I wanted to talk to you alone."

"What's going on Jamel? Is everything okay?"

"Yes, I need to show you this picture."

"Of who?"

"Not of who, of what."

"Okay, what is it?"

Darius looked at Jamel with a huge grin on his face after glancing at the picture.

"Platinum? What, four carats?"

"Damn, you're good!"

"Are you serious, man?"

"Yes, I'm serious. I'm going to propose to her while we're on vacation."

"Wow, man. That's amazing. I'm so happy for you two. Proud of you, man. I knew you wanted to find a good wife, but I wondered if you would because you're so picky."

"Shouldn't I be?"

"Absolutely. You should."

"I'll fill you in on the details before the trip, okay?"

"Sounds good, man. So, she has no clue; huh?"

"Not at all."

"Okay, your secret is safe with me. I won't even tell

Keisha. I promise."

"Thanks, man."

"I'm proud of you, man. For doing things the right way and all."

"Keisha and I had good intentions, but that all changed when we found out that Keyana was on the way."

"It's okay. You're happy, right?"

"Man, I haven't been happier. The love we share can make it through anything. After coming through this, I'm certain of it. I love that woman more than I have ever loved anyone and I will never love another."

"That's deep."

"I mean it, man."

"I know you do."

"We better get over there with the ladies before they start wondering what we're whispering about," said Darius.

"For sure."

The two men took their places next to their ladies to talk about some of the cute things Keyana did while she was staying with them. Jamel knew he wanted to have a couple of kids someday. Now that he was planning their future, he wouldn't have to wait much longer. His life would be complete, but for now, he would enjoy watching his Goddaughter grow up. She was the glue that had strengthened the bond between them, not only as friends for life; but as family.

11 ALL CLEAR

Keisha and Darius waited patiently in the lobby of Dr. Mazzini's office. They were both anxious to find out how Keisha had progressed in her recovery so that they could put another part of the tragic events behind them. Keyana was with both sets of grandparents who were going to lunch together. This was something they'd done often since the wedding. They had been close prior to that, but now were inseparable and took vacations together. Most of all, they loved spending time with the baby.

"Babe, do you think Dr. Mazzini will agree to let me go to Turks & Caicos?"

"I don't see why not. You've done everything that he told you to do. Do you feel up to it? I mean, there's still a whole month before the departure date. I'm guessing you'll feel even better as the weeks go by, but if you think you shouldn't go. We don't have to."

"Oh, no. I actually feel like I could do it now, so I should be feeling 100 percent better by then."

In his mind, he was praying she would be up to it. He knew she would never forgive herself if she missed the proposal. Jamel was one of her best friends, if not her very best friend and he knew she would be disappointed if she missed it.

"Mrs. Kingston?" yelled the physician's assistant as she stood in the lobby wearing purple medical scrubs. "How are you today?" she asked while walking Keisha and Darius back to Dr. Mazzini's triage area to get her vitals.

"I'm well. How are you?"

"Just great. Thanks. I need to get your height and weight," she said while glancing at Darius although she was talking to Keisha.

Keisha stepped onto the scale which revealed that she had lost several pounds over the past few months. She was even thinner than she was in her pre-pregnancy days.

"Wow, babe. You've lost a few pounds," said Darius. He knew that it was more than a few, but he didn't want to upset her.

"That's to be expected after what she's been through. She'll get it back," said the nurse. "Besides, I think she would be a beauty at any size."

"You've got that right," Darius smiled.

"It's not easy chasing a crawling baby all over the house. I'm sure she's contributed to my weight loss," said Keisha.

"I imagine that must be quite the challenge. Why don't you have a seat in the chair next to your husband? I just need to get your blood pressure and temperature."

Keisha followed orders and took a seat next to Darius.

"Your blood pressure is good, and your temperature is 98.4. Okay, please follow me to exam room twelve."

Again, Keisha followed orders; this time with Darius trailing closely behind. He helped her onto the exam table.

"Dr. Mazzini will be with you momentarily. If you need anything prior to that, please let one of the ladies out at the desk know," said the nurse before exiting the room.

"You better be glad you didn't have to disrobe. I might have tried to get a quickie before the doctor came in."

"You're a fool," Keisha laughed.

Darius talked a lot of trash, but most of the time she

knew he was joking. He always had a line or something humorous to say that he thought would lighten the mood. It was one of the reasons why she loved him so much. Not only was he handsome, and the sexiest man she'd ever known. He was funny, too.

"Come in!" Keisha said as a response to the light tap on the door.

"Well hello, Mrs. Kingston. Mr. Kingston? How are you doing these days?"

"Hi, Dr. Mazzini. I'm doing just fine now that I have my beautiful wife back. Thank you for everything you did to make that happen."

"I had very little to do with it. Your wife did most of the work."

"She's definitely a fighter, isn't she?"

In Darius's mind, he agreed with Dr. Mazzini for the most part, but he knew that God had a bigger part in it than anyone else. If not for him, she wouldn't be here.

Dr. Mazzini listened to her heart and examined the area of her head where she was struck. Keisha hadn't complained of any pain or anything since coming home from the hospital. She really seemed to be progressing well.

"Keisha, I'm going to send you next door to have some x-rays and another MRI if you don't mind. I want to get a picture of what's going on in there to make sure that there aren't any areas of concern. This is primarily precautionary after your ordeal. The ligature marks are gone, which is very good. Once I look at the results if everything is good; I won't need to see you for another six months."

"That's great news! How soon will I be able to get the results?"

"You'll get them right after the test. I'm going to have you come back here and I'll review the images with you at that time. You two can head over there now while I put the order in the system."

"Sounds good. Thanks, Dr. Mazzini. We'll see you after the tests."

The technician took a series of images per the doctor's request before giving Keisha the go-ahead to put her personal items and jewelry back on. She and Darius headed back to Dr. Mazzini's office to wait for the results. Though she felt confident that everything was in order, there was still a small amount of worry that crept into her mind.

"Babe, what did I tell you about worrying about stuff. You said you were feeling fine, so we're going to focus on your good health and not think about anything negative."

"You're right, babe. I have to get better about my faith."

As they were hoping, Dr. Mazzini didn't find anything wrong. In fact, the MRI showed Keisha was on a steady path to recovery and wouldn't have any issues as a result of the blow to her head.

"So, it looks like we'll be leaving for Turks & Caicos next month! I'm so excited!"

"Yes, me too, babe. We're going to have a blast. A time that we'll never forget."

"Keisha, I want to talk to you about something," Darius said as they drove back home.

"What's going on?"

"I think we need to go to church. When I met you, you were going to church faithfully. In fact, you were very active. We haven't gone that much, and I think it's time for us to get more consistent about it after everything that God has done to bless us and our family."

"Wow! You know I agree with you. I regret not going like I used to. You're the head of our house and hearing it come from you means so much to me. Yes, we need to get back into the church. I want our daughter to have a strong Christian foundation and it's our responsibility to make sure that she does. Thanks, babe. I must ask, though. What brought this on?"

"Well, I was so afraid of losing you. Even before this whole thing with Stephanie happened. When you broke up with me before, I didn't think I'd ever see you again. Now, look at us. We're a family. Fast forward. We went through some trials that could have taken you away from me forever, but God brought you back. Our family unit is stronger than it's ever been and I'm so thankful. For that, we owe God so much and there's no better way to show him how thankful we are than to study his word and to become spiritually grounded in a church where we can surround ourselves with other Christian families who are also trying to live the right way."

"That's amazing, babe. Yes, we do owe God so much. Our parents are going to be so happy. You know how many times my mom and dad hinted around about this?"

"Yes, I can imagine. It's probably not as much as my parents hinting around about it."

"Well, they'll be happy to know that this was a family decision. We can even invite Jamel and Monica to come with us. What do you think of that?"

"I agree. They're our closest friends and we should share that part of our lives with them too."

"It's settled, then. Sunday, we're going to church."

Darius drove the rest of the way to the house thinking about how much better life would be with God by their sides every step of the way. He knew that God had always been there, but now that their lives were going to move in a more spiritual direction, it was going to be amazing. He just knew it.

12 SUNDAY MORNING

Keisha awoke to the smell of turkey bacon cooking in the kitchen. Darius had gotten out of bed at 5:00 o'clock to get in a quick workout before taking his shower. Now he was at the stove scrambling eggs and flipping bacon wearing nothing but a towel. From the edge of the kitchen, Keisha admired him. They had come a long way since their beginning. Keisha walked up to him and placed her arms securely around his waist. She rested her head on his back.

"This smells delicious, babe."

"I figured we could enjoy a nice breakfast before getting ready for church."

She had no idea how excited he was to be going.

"I made this egg for Keyana. I scrambled it soft like she likes it."

"Okay, I'll get her. I heard her stirring in her crib a couple of minutes ago."

Keisha headed back upstairs to grab the baby before heading back downstairs.

"Daddy made you some eggs," she said.

Keyana smiled and reached for her mother's lips.

"That's right. Do you want to eat? Daddy made us breakfast. He's such a good daddy," Keisha said.

She placed Keyana in her highchair before taking her regular seat right next to her. Darius placed the plates on the table before securing the suction cups on Keyana's plate to the highchair tray. Her chubby fingers reached for her spoon, although she hadn't yet mastered its use.

"Babe, thanks for cooking this," Keisha said before placing a small piece of turkey bacon and a fork full of cheese eggs into her mouth.

Keyana followed suit and placed her empty spoon into her mouth. Realizing she had missed, she grabbed a hand full of eggs with her chubby fingers and placed them into her mouth.

"Yum!" she said.

Keisha and Darius both laughed.

"Man, she's growing up so fast, isn't she?"

"Yes, she sure is. What do you think about having another one?"

"Keisha, I would love to have a whole house full of them, but we have to make sure that you can handle it considering your health and all. Well, maybe not a house full. One more, at least."

"I've been thinking about giving it another try maybe in about a year?"

"Sounds like a plan."

The two of them watched Keyana stuff a small strawberry into her mouth before reaching for more of the eggs. She had a healthy appetite. Cooking for her was always so rewarding because she appreciated good food.

"Babe, I'll bathe Keyana while you take your shower since I've already taken mine."

"Sounds good. I'll lay her outfit out before I get into the shower."

"We'll need to leave here no later than 7:15 to get to the early service. I'll stay here with her while she finishes. You can go ahead and start getting ready if you want."

Keisha stood from the table, giving Darius a tender kiss on the lips before making her exit. Rubbing the top of Keyana's curls, she kissed the top of her head.

13 IN GOD'S HOUSE

Darius glanced at Keisha out of the corner of his right eye before stopping at the light that had just turned red.

"You look amazing, babe."

"You're looking very handsome yourself."

Keisha's hot pink dress with matching pumps were a complement to Darius's grey suit. Keyana wore a cream-colored dress covered with hot pink and lavender flowers with a matching headband. They were a beautiful family. Darius turned to one of the Christian radio stations on his satellite radio. He figured they could start their praise and worship before arriving at the church. Keyana, securely strapped in her car seat began to clap her hands. She had personality. Lots of it.

Darius pulled into the parking lot of the church Keisha had been a part of for so many years prior to meeting Darius. He took the space right next to Monica's car.

"Babe, you didn't tell me Monica and Jamel were joining us!"

"It was a surprise. I talked to Jamel about it the same day we talked about coming."

"I can't believe Monica didn't say anything."

"It was a surprise, remember?"

Monica and Jamel exited the new Mercedes S-Class he'd just purchased for her.

"Girl, why didn't you tell me you two were coming?"

"Darius and Jamel wanted it to be a surprise, so I was sworn to secrecy."

"Well, I'm pleasantly surprised and so happy to see you."

Jamel walked over holding Keyana in his arms. He gave Keisha a kiss on the cheek before taking Monica's hand to head toward the church. Darius placed his arm around Keisha's back and escorted her in the same direction.

"Isn't this great? This is the way life is supposed to be," Keisha smiled at her best friends.

As they entered the sanctuary, the sound of the choir singing, "Miracles" from Kirk Franklin's latest release could be heard throughout the place.

"What an appropriate song to hear after all we've been through. God is good," Keisha admitted.

The four of them took their seats close to the front of the church. Darius took Keyana from Jamel and placed her on his lap. Monica and Keisha stood to join in on the praise and worship part of the service. Jamel and Darius did the same with baby Keyana clapping her hands to the sound of the music. Darius could feel the spirit of the Lord all around him. He hadn't been to church in a while, but he had grown up in the church and therefore recognized it as something very familiar to him. He felt good.

After praise and worship and regular announcements, the pastor took his place on the pulpit to begin his sermon. Today's topic was "Nothing Just Happens." Keisha took notes in her hot pink notebook as the pastor delivered his message. She felt like the message was targeted at her and her family. Despite everything, she had survived. Her family unit was strong, and she was healthy. She couldn't ask for anything more than that. Well, there was one thing. Although she had been living right, she had fallen short in her relationship with

God and wanted to get back to where she was when she and Darius first met. Keisha wanted to rededicate her life to God. So, when it was time for altar call, she stood and headed toward the pulpit with Keyana in her arms. Darius followed. After all, they were a family. They had both been saved and had been living the way married couples should, but there was the period before they were married where they participated in premarital sex, drinking, using profanity, and God only knew what else. Gone were those days. Neither of them was drinking and the sex between them was now as a married couple. The only thing missing was the restoration of their relationship with God and consistently going to church and studying the Bible.

After the pastor prayed over the family and a dozen others who had accepted the altar call, Keisha felt hands on her back. There were Monica and Jamel, and her cousin, Sanai and her husband James. Keisha hadn't noticed them when they entered the church, but here they were standing in support of her and her family. Sanai and James had also been members of Ebenezer AME Church for years. Even though the cousins were close, they hadn't spoken in a while. Keisha grabbed her cousin and hugged her tightly around her neck as tears streamed down her face.

Today was turning out to be a very good day for them all. After service, the group headed to Legal Seafood in Crystal City for an early lunch.

"Keisha, it is so good to see you. I didn't even realize that you were still in the area," said Sanai. "We haven't even seen you at a family reunion in a couple of years."

"Yes, you're right. I've been so busy up until recently."

She brought Sanai and James up to speed on what had been going on in their lives and promised to get better about staying in touch. It looked like they would at least be seeing each other each Sunday in church but hoped to spend more time together regularly. Before leaving the restaurant, they took a few pictures to capture the day.

"I'm going to call you in a few days to check on you," Sanai promised.

"Girl, you know where I'll be. I love you."

"I love you too."

Sanai and James headed down the street toward their car while the others headed in the opposite direction toward their vehicles.

"So, what are you guys doing with the rest of your day?" Monica asked.

"We're just heading to the house. I'm going to change into something more comfortable and just relax. What about you two?"

"I spoke to Cynthia last night. She wants to come by, so I'll probably hang out with her for a little bit. Maybe we'll stop by if you're up to it."

"Yes, that would be great! I haven't seen her in a little while. We need to catch up."

"Okay, so we'll see you in a couple of hours. I'll shoot you a text when we're on the way."

"Sounds good."

Keisha and Monica hugged before she got into the car.

"Babe, do you need to go anywhere before we head back to the house?"

"No, I'm good. Thanks, though."

"Service was good, wasn't it?"

"Yes, it sure was. I'm so glad we decided to go. I can't wait to see what God has in store for us. Life is going to be even better than it was before," said Darius.

"We'll get better about handling adversities, although we've done a pretty good job so far; there's always room for improvement."

"You got that right. What do you think about putting Keyana down for a nap when we get to the house so that we can watch a movie before Monica and Cynthia get there?"

"Sounds like a plan."

Keisha rested her eyes while Darius drove them back home. She was a little tired but excited inside to know that she was back in good graces with God. She couldn't wait to share the news with her parents.

14 UNEXPECTED GUESTS

Darius slowly pulled into the driveway but hesitated before opening the garage door. The unfamiliar black Dodge Charger with dark tint parked in front of the house made him cautious.

"Keisha, do you know who that is?"

"No, I don't recognize the vehicle."

"You stay here, I'll be right back."

He jumped out of the car, locking the doors behind him. Darius walked over to the Dodge as the window came down. Keisha looked out of the side mirror as Darius spoke to the driver.

The man exited the vehicle and the two talked for a couple of minutes before Darius headed back to his vehicle to help Keisha and Keyana into the house. He rubbed his hand across the back of his head which raised concern with Keisha. Darius only did that when he was troubled by something.

"Babe, what's going on?"

"Can you do me a favor, Babe? Why don't you go ahead and put Keyana down for that nap? I'll tell you about it in a minute."

Darius unlocked the front door and handed her Keyana

who was already asleep.

"Trust me, Babe. After you put Keyana down, please meet me in the family room."

Keisha did as she was told, although her nerves were getting the best of her; she trusted her husband and knew that Darius wouldn't let anything happen to her. After laying Keyana in her crib, she removed her dress and headband before placing her blanket over her legs. She placed her stuffed bumble bee on the blanket. It would be the first thing Keyana looked for upon awakening.

Keisha heard the echo of the unfamiliar voice and her husband as she headed down the stairs and into the family room.

"Babe, this is Antonio."

"Hi, Antonio. What's going on?" she asked as she looked at Darius for the answer.

There was a little girl about a year old sitting closely at his side. She was so close that her head was pressed against Antonio's arm.

"Keisha, please sit," Darius patted the cushion right next to him.

"Hi, Keisha. I hate to disturb the two of you with this, but I thought you needed to know," said Antonio.

"Needed to know what?" Keisha looked at Darius before focusing her attention back on Antonio.

"I'm Stephanie's boyfriend. We dated for a little over a year. In fact, we were dating up until her death."

"Oh, okay. Antonio, I'm really sorry about what happened."

"Thank you, but Stephanie was wrong to do what she did. She was sick and had been for a while. She was under the care of a psychiatrist, but she wasn't consistent with her visits or the medication. Unfortunately, she had to suffer the consequences of her actions. That doesn't dismiss the fact that I miss her every day, though."

Darius took Keisha's hand, "Babe, there's something I need to tell you."

"Darius, what is it?"

"Keisha, Stephanie told Antonio that I might be the father of this little girl. Her name is Daria. She's Stephanie's daughter."

"Wait a minute. What?"

"Keisha, I had no idea that there was a child. I never knew she was pregnant. I really didn't."

"Keisha, he's telling the truth. He didn't know."

"Oh my God, Darius. What next?" Keisha began to cry.

"Babe, please listen to me. I didn't know. I told you, I used protection when I had sex with her. It was only one time. I never lied about that!"

Daria sat on the edge of the chair looking from Darius to Keisha and then to Antonio. The poor child had no idea what was going on, but it was certain that she'd been through a lot if she'd been living with Stephanie for the past year.

"Antonio, you understand that I'm going to want to get a paternity test, right?"

"Yes, by all means. I understand. I thought I was her father until I decided to get tested. It would be smart to do so."

Keisha wiped her tears and took a deep breath.

"Yes, we definitely need to get this done as soon as possible. I'm sorry, but this news is just very upsetting. Just as soon as I feel like things are getting back on track, now this. It's just too much."

Keisha looked at Daria with her light brown eyes and jet-black curls. She was a pretty little girl. She couldn't help but feel sorry for her. Her entire world had been turned upside down. Not only did she lose her mother, but she was probably about to lose the only man who had been familiar to her. The one who'd been there for her since the day she was born. There was a sadness in her eyes. Almost as if she knew what she was facing, even though she was only eleven months old.

"I'll see if I can get an appointment for tomorrow. We need to get this issue resolved as soon as possible. Where do you live, man?"

"We flew in from Atlanta yesterday. If you could get tested this week, that would be great. I took the week off in hopes of getting this done although I know it could be a while before we get the results back, I can at least get back to work while we wait."

"So, what's the plan?"

"Well, Daria and I will head back to Atlanta at the end of the week. Once the results come in, we can figure this all out. As far as I'm concerned, I'm her father. I've been raising her since the moment she was born. I love this little girl. Finding out that I wasn't the father was the worst news I'd ever received. It was even worse than finding out that Stephanie was gone. I know that sounds weird, but it's true. She took me through a lot too while we were together. I guess this is the grand finale."

"Yes, I bet it is."

"Anyway, here's my card. We're staying at the Courtyard Marriott in Waldorf. Please call me when you find out when the appointment will be, and I'll meet you at the office with Daria. If the results come back positive, we'll need to talk about what you want to do. The truth is, I can't stand the thought of losing her, but she's not my daughter. If she's yours, the decision will be up to you."

"I hear you, man. Well, thanks for getting in touch with me about this. I've got some damage control to do with my wife."

Keisha had made her way into the kitchen where she was sitting at the table in silence. They had been through so much. How could this be happening? Then she remembered today's sermon. Nothing just happens. At that moment, she lifted her head and went back into the family room where Antonio stood holding Daria. Keisha walked up to the little girl and ran her fingers through her beautiful curls.

"We'll get through this, Darius. We will. Antonio, is there anything that I can get you and Daria?"

"Well, I could use a bottle of water. We were waiting out there for a while before you came home."

Keisha headed back to the kitchen and grabbed a bottle of water and an apple juice drink box from the refrigerator. She pierced the small foil insert with the straw before handing it to Daria, then she handed Antonio the bottle of water.

"This will all work itself out," she said.

Rubbing the baby's arm, she smiled. It was all she could do to keep from crying again, but the tears weren't for the situation they were now facing. She felt sadness for the motherless child.

15 UNCONDITIONAL LOVE

Darius walked Antonio and Daria back to the car. Keisha watched intently from the front porch. She couldn't believe what had just transpired but recognized it as something that had the potential to shake their marriage from its foundation if she let it. Keisha wouldn't do it. She loved her husband so much that she knew in her heart that she would stand with him through this, regardless of the test results. It's a good thing she was all prayed up.

"Baby, I am so sorry," Darius grabbed Keisha in his arms after stepping up onto the porch. "I really had no idea."

"I know you didn't. It's okay. I expect that you'll be on the phone first thing in the morning making that appointment, though."

"Yes, I will."

"Well, there's no point in focusing too much on it until we know for certain, right?"

"You're right."

"So, let's just get back to life as usual until we know. Monica and Cynthia will be coming over in a little while. I'm not going to mention anything about this to anyone until we know. Is that okay with you?"

"Yes, babe. It is. I love you, you know that?"

"I do. I love you too, Darius."

The couple walked back into the house together and headed upstairs to change clothes before Cynthia and Monica arrived.

"You might want to tell Monica to bring Jamel. I could really use his company right about now while you guys talk."

"Okay, I will."

After changing clothes, Keisha headed into the kitchen to gather some snacks for the visit. She made a cheese, cracker, and pepperoni tray. Then she poured some mixed nuts into a small bowl. As she walked around the kitchen, she couldn't help but wonder why they were being tested so much, but she recognized that God was in control and as a result, he would see them through. She was removing the plastic lid from the shrimp cocktail Darius had bought at Costco the day before when the doorbell rang.

"This better be the guys. I can't take any more surprises," she said.

"You got that right, babe. I can't either."

The trio headed into the foyer after Keisha opened the door.

"What's wrong with you? You look like you've been crying, "Monica asked.

"I'm okay. I've just been running around trying to get ready for you guys. Come on in."

Keisha headed toward the family room with her friends following closely behind.

"Where's Darius?" Jamel looked at Monica and shrugged his shoulders. He wasn't sure what was going on but didn't like it.

"He'll be down in a minute," she said. "Cynthia, I haven't seen you in a while. How are you?"

"I'm doing okay. You look amazing! I can't even tell you've been through anything."

"Thank God I don't look like what I've been through,

trust me."

"Thank God none of us do, right?"

"Amen."

Jamel walked to the edge of the staircase, "Darius, I'll be in the basement, man!"

"Okay! Be right down!"

He kissed Monica on her forehead before leaving them to talk.

"Keisha, you sure you're okay?"

"Girl, yeah. I'm fine. So, what's going on with you, Cynthia?" She changed the subject.

"I've been so busy! Between decorating the house and work, I haven't had much time for anything else."

"Have you heard from Rico anymore since he wrote to you? Monica mentioned it. I hope you don't mind."

"No, I don't mind at all. Yes, he called me about a week ago."

"Please tell me you didn't accept his call?"

"Actually, I did. I needed some closure on that situation."

Keisha looked at Monica before focusing her attention back on Cynthia.

"So, what did he have to say?"

"He just kept apologizing for what he did. He said he was sorry for hurting me. You too, Monica."

"I really don't need his apology. I'm glad he hasn't reached out to me. I want to forget he ever existed."

"Well, after his apology; he went on to tell me how much he hates it in prison. He said he couldn't wait to get out."

"Is he serious? He's got a long time before that'll be happening."

"He seems to think he'll be out in a couple of years. But get this. He had the nerve to ask me to come for a visit."

"Well, what did you say to that?"

"I told him it would be a cold day in hell before I did that. If that wasn't enough, he then asked me to send him some money."

"You have got to be kidding me!"

"No, I wish I was. Anyway, I told him that I wouldn't be doing that either. I did agree to call his mother to let her know that he needed to see her. Then I hung up. Oh, I called you earlier from my new number. Please program it in your phone. I changed it after I called his mother."

"That's what I'm talking about. He's such a user!" said Monica.

"I'm so glad all of that is over. I couldn't be in a better place in my life than where I am right now. I'm in a loving and healthy relationship with the man of my dreams. Jamel is so good to me, I can't even believe it. Sometimes, I feel like I'm dreaming."

"I'm glad you two are doing well," Keisha said as her mind wandered to the new drama she and Darius were now facing. "Cynthia, there's someone out there for you too. Trust me."

"Jamel said Darius invited us to an air traffic controller event next weekend. Maybe we can get a ticket for Cynthia to come too?"

"You know, that's an excellent idea. I'll make sure that it happens."

"No, I really don't want to be a fifth wheel. You guys go ahead and have a great time."

"Girl, do you know how many eligible bachelors will be at this event? You better grab your sexiest little black dress and come! It's not optional. It's mandatory."

"Keisha's right. We went last year and there were a lot of single men there. You don't have to go with the idea of finding a man in the back of your mind. Let's just go and have a good time. If you find one, you find one. How about that?"

"No, if one finds her, then he finds her! How about that?" Keisha asked.

"You've got that right, okay, I'm in."

"Well, it's settled."

"Monica said you guys had a great time in church today. I've been to that church a couple of times. I really enjoyed myself too. That pastor always has a powerful message. I've been to churches where I just didn't feel spiritually fed, but I've never felt like that over there. I'll have to come again."

"Yes, you should definitely do that if you feel the spirit of the Lord moving through the place whenever you go. I sure felt it. In fact, the enemy is always busy trying to steal your joy, so you must have a good place to worship to stay spiritually grounded. I'm not trying to talk like I've been in the church every Sunday or that I've been reading my Bible every day because that hasn't been me in a very long time. However, I recognize where I've fallen short and I'm trying to bring it back together now. Attending church today wasn't an accident. It was intentional and right on time. It was what I needed. Darius too."

"Yeah, she's right, Cynthia. Jamel and I needed it too. It's time for us all to be more consistent about our relationships with God."

"You guys are right. After what I've been through, I really need to get back into a good church. God has been good to me. The situation that I went through . . . that we went through with Rico could have turned out a lot worse than it did. I recognize that, and I owe it all to God. Count me in. I'll be there next Sunday."

"Yes! I'm very happy now. God loves us. Flaws and all. His love is unconditional. When I think about all the things I've done wrong in my life and how he never left me, it makes me emotional. No matter what we do, he's still there. Unconditional love is an amazing thing. It's how Darius and I love each other. Unconditionally. I guess you could say, we're learning from God."

"You're right. I love Jamel the same way and he loves me like that. Think about it. What kind of a man gets involved in a relationship with a woman like me, knowing what I've been through?"

"A good one," said Keisha. "A Godly man. You deserve him. You're a good person with a kind heart. Just because you went through something with Rico, doesn't make you bad and you're not damaged. Please stop saying that."

"You're right. I need to stop. I just can't believe that my life has taken this turn for the better. For the amazing! I couldn't be happier than I am right now."

"Well, just sit back and enjoy the ride. Jamel is an amazing person and I'm sure he has nothing but the best in store for you. He couldn't have ended up with a better person, Monica."

"I'm excited about my future. I've never been excited about my future before, but now I wake up with excitement in my heart. I thank God for Jamel."

"He thanks God for you too, every day. We've talked about it. He loves you so much. I've never seen him this way with anyone and I mean that. You should know. You've known him almost as long as I have, remember?"

"Yeah, you're right. I want to get married someday and give him lots of babies. Two or three at least."

"He wants that too. That's why I know you two are perfect for each other. You both want the same things. You'll get it too. Wait and see."

Cynthia marinated on Keisha's words to Monica. She wanted it too but knew it would have to be in God's time. She knew she was also a good person and had a lot to offer, but she would never settle for the wrong man ever again. If it meant waiting, she would just have to do it. After all, she wasn't the most religious person in the world, but she knew that she need not seek out her perfect man. According to God's word, he would find her; and she believed that then and only then would it be God's will and not something that God allowed to happen because she forced it.

Keisha headed down to the basement to take the men some snacks. Suddenly, she knew that the current situation that she and Darius were facing was going to be okay.

"All things are working for our good," she said silently and inhaled. "It's going to be okay."

16 A WOMAN OF GOD

Keisha sat in her chair in front of the vanity staring at her image in the mirror. Darius noticed the seriousness of her expression as he stood behind her gazing at her beautiful image. She looked physically and emotionally exhausted. Neither of them had shared the news that Darius might have fathered a child with Stephanie. It was something they would reserve for later discussions after the results were in.

"Babe, are you okay?" he asked.

"Yes. Just thinking."

"You wanna talk about it?"

"No, I'm good. Just tired."

Darius knew that she was keeping something from him, but figured it was just concerning the drama they were going through. He didn't want Daria to be his daughter. He didn't want any reminders of what he had been through with Stephanie. He never cared about her and definitely never loved her. On the other hand, there was a little girl out there who had no mother and if he was her father he was going to have to do right by her. He was going to have to pay for what he'd done. It's amazing how one night of sex could have the potential to ruin your entire life.

Keisha was a good woman. She was determined to stand by her man no matter what the outcome. After all, she'd taken a vow to be with him through the good and the bad until the end of time and she meant it. She knew it wouldn't be easy but they would make it, if it was in God's will for them to raise Daria.

Immediately, she thought of what her friends would think. What would her parents think? What would Darius's parents think? There was so much to think about. How would she explain to strangers that the two children weren't twins because they were so close in age?

"Why am I even thinking about this when we don't even know the outcome yet?" she asked out loud.

"Babe, did you say something?"

"I was talking to myself."

"Keisha, please talk to me."

"Darius, I'm not even sure what to say right now."

"Do you still love me?"

"Of course, I love you. That'll never change. We took a vow, remember? I was serious about everything I said on our wedding day. Now don't get me wrong. I'm no fool, but what happened between the two of you happened when we weren't together. It's unfortunate, but it could have happened to anyone."

"Yeah. I just wish it hadn't happened to us."

"I get that, but nothing just happens. Remember that, Darius."

"You're right. Let's just go to bed. I'm going to check on Keyana. I'll be right back."

Darius picked Keyana up from her crib and placed her on the changing table. He could tell that she needed to be changed.

"Dadada," she said.

Darius smiled at his little princess with the chubby cheeks. She melted his heart every time he looked at her. He picked her up and held her tightly to his chest. The tears began to fill his eyes as he remembered the day she was born. What a blessing. Then he remembered the image of Stephanie standing in the doorway of Keisha's hospital room. She was out of her mind. He never realized how crazy she was and wished that he'd never attached himself to her by engaging in a sexual encounter that now may have bonded them together forever, even though she was no longer alive.

After kissing Keyana on her cheek, he returned her to her crib and covered her legs with the blanket.

"I love you, little angel."

"Dadada. Dadada," she babbled.

Darius smiled at her one last time before turning off the light. When he returned to their master suite, he found Keisha fast asleep. He couldn't help but feel sadness as he watched her. She didn't deserve this. Since they'd been together, she'd endured things that she should never have had to go through. She was a good woman. The best thing that had ever happened to him. Darius knew that they had come out on the other side of some of their struggles and believed they could get through this. He would just have to continue to pray about it.

Darius began to reminisce about some of the things he'd done in his past. He hadn't been a good person before meeting Keisha. The truth is, he was a womanizer. He'd had lots of sex with lots of women and none of it meant anything to him. He did it because he could. He was a good-looking man and women threw themselves at him. He had been around, but Keisha changed him. He knew the moment he met her that he wanted to spend the rest of his life with her. He was ready to stop having meaningless sex with multiple women and wanted to share the intimacy with her. No one else. Now, he was possibly going to have to pay for his indiscretions. He knew that Keisha had saved him from himself. Perhaps, she'd even saved his life.

17 WHO'S YOUR DADDY?

It had been several weeks since Darius and Daria underwent the paternity test. He had been in contact with Antonio at least a couple of times a week to see how she was doing. He even offered to send money, but Antonio didn't need it. Darius learned that he had his own business down in Atlanta. A very successful one. He owned his own home and was a good dude just trying to do the right thing by a little girl who had no one.

Darius inhaled and exhaled after he pulled the envelope out of the mailbox that would reveal what their future might look like. He headed into the house to look for Keisha.

"Babe, the results are here!"

Keisha came downstairs with Keyana in her arms. Although she said she wouldn't worry, she couldn't help but feel overwhelmed at that moment. They had asked God to help them to accept his will, and that's what they would do.

They sat down on the sofa in the family room. Darius pulled the letter out of the envelope. He read it intently. Keisha looked on but didn't say a word. She didn't need to. The tears in Darius's eyes painted the picture of what was written on the other side of the paper.

"Babe, I am so sorry," he cried. "She's my daughter."

Keisha placed Keyana in her play yard before sitting back down next to Darius. She began to sob, but not because she knew the truth. She sobbed because her husband was in pain. How could they return to any sense of normalcy after this? Daria was only four months older than Keyana. Imagine the stares from people who knew them.

"Darius, it's okay. I was hoping that the results would be different, but it is what it is. She's your daughter and she needs her father. That little girl . . . your daughter doesn't have a mother. She's already been through so much."

"You're right. I guess I better call Antonio to let him know the news."

"I'll be upstairs. I'm going to place Keyana down for a nap. I'll give you some time to talk to him."

Keisha held Keyana closely and headed to the nursery. She placed her in her crib. Looking down at her beautiful daughter, she brushed the light-colored curls lining her hairline with her fingers. Smiling, she silently thanked God for her. As she turned to walk away, the tears began to fall from both cheeks. Keisha couldn't deny the fact that she was also hurt. Darius's indiscretions had brought them to this place. A place she wished they could both escape unscathed, but the reality was Daria. How would this all play out? When would she come to live with them?

"Wow! This is too much," she said out loud while heading to the rocking chair in Keyana's room.

Keisha picked up the small white Bible her mother had given Keyana as a gift the day she was born. She turned to 1 Peter 5:7. It was what she needed at that moment. Then she read Philippians 4:7. The spirit of the Lord led her there. Before she knew it, an hour had passed.

Darius stood in the doorway watching his wife as she read.

"Babe, I didn't even hear you come up," she said.

"You were so engaged in God's word that I didn't want to disturb you."

"So, how did your conversation with Antonio go?"

"As good as it could, I guess. He's upset because he doesn't want to have to give her up."

"I can understand that. So, what are you guys going to do about this?"

"Well, I told him I needed to talk to you about everything first."

"Darius, this has nothing to do with me. You have to do what's best for you and Daria."

"Keisha, what are you trying to say? Are you bailing out on me? I thought you said you were in this with me."

"I did say that, and I meant it. The thing is, this transition will need to be as seamless as possible for the baby. She's been through a lot. Not to mention, Antonio is the only father she's known since the day she was born. This is going to be difficult for him also. You have to consider those things."

"But what about you? This is going to have an effect on you too. You and Keyana."

"Don't worry about her. She won't even remember any of this later. Daria probably won't either."

"Okay, well what about you?"

"Darius, I have to admit that this is a little troubling; but it's in God's hands. I must keep telling myself that. He's going to see us through. We're in this together. Daria not only needs you, but she's going to need a mother too. Although the situation isn't ideal, it's what we have."

Keisha knew that she was going to have to stay prayed up about it. Thank goodness, Daria didn't look much like Stephanie because that could make it more difficult. She did have Darius's features. She was as cute as she could be. Not that Stephanie wasn't attractive too, in her own way.

"So, when do you think she'll be coming to live with us?"

"I think we're going to have to take it slow. I don't want to shock her by having Antonio snatched away from her so soon after losing her mother. Besides, he did say that he wanted to continue to have a relationship with her. Maybe summer visits and things like that. He asked if it was okay if he came to Maryland to visit her from time to time. I don't have a problem with it. What do you think? I mean, what about her staying in Atlanta? This is all so confusing. What a mess I've made."

"Well, this has to be hard for him. So, yes, I agree that he should have as much contact with her as necessary to make the transition go as smoothly as possible. Darius, you must also recognize that Antonio is probably going to want to be a part of her life for the rest of her life. You can't expect him to just walk away from this. As far as her staying with him, that's up to you. The question is, could you live with that? Knowing that another man is raising your daughter? I'm just saying."

"We have so much to do. We're going to have to order a new birth certificate. I guess I better contact our attorney, but we have a lot of explaining to do even before we get to that point. Keisha, I don't know what to do or what to think right now. I need to marinate on all of this."

"Yes, I understand that, and yes we have a lot to do."

Darius picked up the phone and dialed his parents' phone number.

"Hi, son. How are you?" asked Candace.

"I'm okay, Mom. Is Dad at home?"

"Yes, he's here. What's going on, Darius?"

"We were going to stop by. I just wanted to make sure you were both going to be home."

"Yes, we're here. Are you sure you're okay? How's Keisha and my grandbaby? Is it DJ? I haven't seen or heard from him in a while."

"No, they're all fine. Mom, we'll be there in about an hour. Is that okay?"

"Well, of course, it is."

"We'll see you in a bit."

"Okay, son."

"Well, I guess we better use Mom and Dad as practice. We're going to have to tell this story a few times whether she comes to live here or not, so we might as well start with them."

Keisha picked her sleeping daughter up from the crib

after putting her sweater on.

"You're right, Darius. We might as well get my parents out of the way too. I'll call them from the car."

The family drove in silence to deliver news that they knew would be difficult, but it had to be done. There was no point in prolonging the inevitable. Life had a way of handing out lemons. It was all about what you did with them that was important.

18 THE TRUTH SHALL SET YOU FREE

Keisha dialed her parent's number to break the silence that filled the car. She and Darius agreed to head over to their home after leaving his parents' house.

"Hey, Mom."

"Hey, Sweetie. How are you?"

"I'm okay. Darius and I wanted to know if we could stop by there in a couple of hours. We're headed to see his parents for a little while and then we'll be there. Are you and Dad going to be home?"

"Yes, we'll be here. Is everything okay?"

"Yes, we just need to talk to you about something."

"Well, okay dear. I don't like the sound of your voice, but okay."

"Don't worry Mom. We'll be there soon."

Darius pulled into the driveway just as Keisha was ending the call.

"Wait, babe."

"What's wrong, Keisha?"

"Lord, please help us find the proper words to say when we explain this situation to our parents. Help us deliver the message in a peaceful way so that our families and friends won't worry but will realize that it is the right thing to do. Daria needs a family and Darius is her father. Therefore, we believe it is your will for her to be a part of our family and for me to raise her like she is my own daughter. Amen."

"Amen," said Darius.

He got out of the car and grabbed Keyana from her car seat before opening the door for Keisha.

"Babe, this is going to be okay. I believe it."

"Thank you for being so understanding. I was so scared that you were going to leave me."

"Darius, what did I tell you? We're in this together. It's not an ideal situation, but it's what we have. Don't ever forget that."

"Yeah, you're right. I love you, baby cakes."

"I love you too. We'd better get in there. I see your Mom looking out the window."

"Hey there. You guys better come on in here and bring me my grandbaby," Candace took Keyana from Darius and kissed her on her cheek.

"Hello to you too, Mom."

"Hi, Son. Hi Keisha. You guys okay?"

"Yeah, we're fine. Where's Dad?"

"I'm in here, son!"

Darius and Keisha headed to the kitchen with Candace trailing closely behind, holding Keyana in her arms.

"I hope you guys are hungry. When your mother said you were coming over, I came in here and whipped up some food for our souls."

"Dad, you might not have an appetite after you find out why we're here."

"What do you mean, Darius? What's going on?"

"Well, about a month or so ago we received a visit from a young man out of Atlanta. He was Stephanie's ex-boyfriend."

"What in the world did he want?"

"Well, you both knew that Stephanie and I had a brief encounter with one another. A one-night stand, pretty much."

"Darius, please don't tell me that you caught something from her."

"No, Mom. It's not like that. It turns out that Stephanie became pregnant from that one sexual encounter. She never said anything."

"Go on, Darius. What are you trying to say?"

"Well, when Antonio showed up, he had a little girl with him. It turns out that the little girl, Daria is the product of the one night stand we had."

"Darius, please tell me you're joking. Please!"

"Mom, I wish I was. The paternity test results just came back, and she is my daughter," he said while handing Candace the paper.

Candace scanned the document. She looked at Darius, and then at Keisha before placing her hands on her forehead.

"This is unbelievable. This woman is never going away, is she?"

"Mom, I'm so sorry. I never intended for this to happen, but I guess it's the consequence I'm having to deal with because of that one night."

"I suppose you're right," said John. "So, what are you going to do?"

"I'm going to have to do what's right."

"Keisha, how do you feel about all of this?"

"Mom, it is what it is. I love my husband and I vowed to stand by him for better or worse. I have to admit, I'm not happy about it, but we have to do it."

"This is definitely worse," Candace reached for Keisha's hand. "I'm so sorry you're having to deal with all this."

"It's okay, Mom. It's not like he cheated on me. God will see us through. I truly believe that. I've been praying, daily."

"You're right, dear. He'll see you both through it. So, when is all of this going to take place? I'm assuming she's coming to live with you, right?"

"Yes, Mom. Well, I believe that's what will happen, but I'm not sure yet. If the decision is for her to come, then yes, she'll be coming to live with us. We're currently trying to work it all out with Antonio."

"That poor man. Did he think that he was the father?"

"Yes, he did up until he knew that he wasn't. He said Stephanie had told him he was."

"Well, it has to be a lot for him to deal with too. You'll have to consider all of that before you bring her here."

"Do you have any pictures of her?"

"No, I don't."

"I do," said Keisha. "I took it when she visited with Antonio."

"Wow. I didn't realize."

"Yes, while she was drinking her juice box. Here she is." Keisha handed her phone to Candace who looked patiently before handing it to John.

"She's a little cutie too. Just like Keyana. Darius, she does look like you."

"Yes, I see the resemblance. I was in denial when I first saw her, but she does look like me. The dark hair, the eyes; even her nose."

"How about you guys eat something. I'm sure you probably haven't been doing that considering all you've been dealing with. Keisha, you need to keep your strength up."

"Dad, you're right. Yes, I could use a little something. What do you have?"

"I made some barbecued chicken, macaroni and cheese, fresh green beans, and cornbread. You want some?"

"As a matter of fact, I would love some. It smells delicious!"

Keisha stood from her seat and headed toward the stove. She felt as if a burden had been lifted from her shoulders. Although she knew they had to approach the issue with her parents, she felt that Candace and John were the most difficult. After all, Daria is their granddaughter.

"Darius, do you want me to fix you a plate?"

"Well, if you're going to eat; I suppose I better do the same. Keyana might be a little hungry too."

Darius pulled Keyana's highchair closer to the table

before Keisha attached the small plate to the tray to make it stationary. She was at the stage of throwing her plate or cup from the tray. He put Keyana in the seat and placed the spoon in her hand. Keyana looked at the spoon in her right hand before grabbing a green bean with the left. She shoved it in her mouth. Keisha returned to the table with plates for her and Darius.

"Mom, Dad? Are you guys going to eat?"

"Of course, we are," Candace headed to the kitchen to fix plates for her and John. "We can't let this news break us. Babies are a gift from God. The circumstances that brought her here are a little different, but she's here now. We just have to figure out how to make the best of this situation, right?"

"You're right, Mom. Thanks for being so understanding. You too, Dad. I thank God for my beautiful wife. I don't know what I would do if she wasn't okay with this," Darius continued.

"Honey, would you bless the food?"

"Dear Lord, thank you for this delicious meal that we're about to receive. Thank you for my son, daughter-in-law, and beautiful granddaughter. Lord, we ask you to help us to get through this situation that has been presented to our family. We believe that love endures all things. Keisha is a very strong woman and we know that you have your hands all over her. It takes a very special person to deal with difficult situations and she is that person. We ask you to bless this family and keep them close to you. These blessings we ask in the name of the Father, the Son, and the Holy Spirit. Amen."

The group said amen in unison before they began to eat the delicious meal that had been prepared for them. Darius reached for Keisha's hand and held it tightly. She smiled at him, and at that moment he knew that they were going to make it through.

19 GOD WILL SEE US THROUGH

Darius pulled into the driveway of his in-law's house. He exhaled before turning off the car.

"Here we go again."

"Well, we made it through the toughest part. It'll be okay, babe."

"Keisha, thank you again. I don't know what I would do without you."

"Well, thank God for you; you don't have to find out," she reached for his hand and held it tightly.

Darius pulled Keisha's hand toward his lips and kissed it gently, "Yes, thank God for that."

"I guess we better go ahead and get this over with."

Darius held Keyana in one arm with his other wrapped around Keisha's waist. She tapped lightly on the door.

"Hey, baby!" Sarah grabbed Keyana from Darius's arms.

"Hi, Sweetie. Darius." She kissed them both on the cheek before stepping aside so they could enter the foyer.

"Hey, Darius. Hey, baby girl. How's it going?

"We're doing okay. We just left my parents' house and

thought we should also pay you two a visit."

"Well, I could tell by Keisha's tone that something's going on so let's get to it. What's going on, you two?"

"Do you mind if we sit down first, Mom?"

"By all means. Let's have a seat in the family room. You guys want anything? Something to drink?"

"No, we're fine. We just had dinner with my parents, so we're good. We had plenty to eat and drink with them."

"Darius, do you want me to start or do you want to do it?"

"I better do it."

"Somebody needs to tell us something. Come on now," said Marcus. "What is it?"

"Okay. Mom and Dad? We came over here to talk to you about something that recently happened."

"We're listening."

"I found out that Stephanie had a daughter, and I'm her father."

"What are you saying, Darius? What in the world?"

"Yes, a little over a month ago a man named Antonio showed up at our house with a little girl just a few months older than Keyana. He said he was Stephanie's boyfriend. Sometime after Daria was born, he found out that he wasn't her father."

Keisha pulled the letter from her purse and handed it to her mother who read it line by line before handing it back. She then handed it to her father.

"So, what are you going to do?" asked Marcus.

"Well, Dad. I'm going to have to do the right thing. Eventually, she's going to have to come to live with us. I believe that's what I need to do. I'm really confused. Right now, we're trying to work through the details. She's down in Atlanta living with Antonio in the only home she's known. She's young, so I'm hoping she won't be too negatively impacted by any of this. If we decide to bring her here."

"Keisha, how are you feeling about all of this?"

"Mom, I have to be okay with it. I love Darius and we'll

make it through. It's a lot to deal with, that's for sure, but my love for him is much stronger than this issue. We'll be okay. We're going to have to lean on God, and probably you two as well. Now, there are going to be two little ones running around. I truly believe that's what's about to happen."

"Keisha, do you think you're physically up to it?"

"Dad, I've made it through much worse things than this. It may even make me stronger than I ever thought I could be. Daria needs her father, and she's going to need a mother too."

"Well, what about Antonio? He's been the one raising her. You know it is probably going to be hard for him to let her go. Do you even know that he's going to?"

"He doesn't exactly have to let her go," said Darius. "I have no problem with him being an active part of her life if he wants to do that. It might be better for Daria anyway. He's familiar to her. We're strangers, at least for now."

"As long as you two can keep your family unit strong and intact, then I'm okay with it. We'll be praying for you two."

"Thanks, Mom. That's all we're asking. We just need your continued love and support, and lots of prayers."

"Keisha, I know you always wanted to have two children. Now you have them."

"Mom, I still want to have another one. It just might be a while. A few years at least."

Darius could feel a little disappointment coming from his wife. His heart ached for what she was going through.

"Well Mom, we better get Keyana home. It's way past her bedtime."

"Okay, well thank you for letting us know what was going on. Remember, we're here for you Sweetie. Both of you. If you need anything, you know you can count on us."

Keisha hugged both of her parents before picking Keyana up from the blanket she was resting on.

"Darius, you keep your head up, Son. We love you very much and know that you'll be a great father to Daria just like you are to Keyana. You'll both be what that little girl needs."

Keisha leaned back on the headrest during the ride home.

Now, they just needed to tell Monica and Jamel. The rest of the crew would also need to know, but Monica and Jamel were a priority over everyone else because they were their closest friends. They were also Keyana's godparents and had now just inherited another goddaughter if they would have her.

"How do you think that went?" Darius asked.

"It went as well as it could have, I suppose. My parents love you, Darius. They've always been very supportive of everything when it comes to us."

"Yeah, I guess you're right. It's a lot to take in."

"They'll be fine. I'm just glad that they know now. I wasn't sure how it was going to go and wasn't looking forward to telling them, but it's done."

"We can worry about Jamel and Monica tomorrow. I've had enough for one day. What do you think?"

"I agree. Tomorrow will be better."

Keisha closed her eyes and had a silent talk with God while Darius drove the rest of the way home. She just wanted to keep a loving heart toward Daria and didn't want to let there be any tension between her and Darius about any of this. One thing she knew for certain is that love did endure all things. Their love was being tested and she would do everything she could to make sure they passed with flying colors.

20 GODDAUGHTERS

Keisha wondered how Monica and Jamel would take the news. After all, they signed up to be Keyana's godparents and would also be godparents to any other children they had. This was a little different. They were not only about to find out that Darius fathered a child with Stephanie, but Monica was going to have to face the reality that she's the one who took her mother's life. How would she take that?

"Well, here we go," said Keisha as she headed to the door to let Monica and Jamel in. Darius waited nervously in the family room.

"Hey, you. What's going on?" Monica asked.

"I'm okay. How are you, lady?"

"I'm doing okay too. What's wrong?"

"Monica, I'm fine. Hey, Jamel."

Jamel leaned in and kissed Keisha on the cheek, "you sure you're okay?"

"Yes, you guys come on in. Can I get you something to drink?"

"No, not yet. We're good for now."

"Hey Darius, man. What's going on?"

"Not much. Well, a lot actually. No need to beat around the bush with a bunch of small talk. I have something to talk to you two about."

"Okay," Jamel took his place on the love seat next to Monica.

"We wanted you two to come over because something life altering has happened, and we wanted to tell you before it was too late."

"Too late for what?" Monica looked from Darius to Keisha, and then to Jamel.

"Stephanie had a child," he paused. "A little girl a few months before Keyana was born. It turns out that I'm her father."

"What? Darius, what in the hell are you talking about?" Monica stood and walked over to the sofa. She took a seat next to Keisha.

"We found out that there was a possibility that I was her father several weeks ago. We found out for certain the other day. I received the test results. There's no question about it."

"A baby? With Stephanie? I'm not believing this!"

Monica was heated. All she could think about was what her friend must be feeling.

"Keisha, how are you? Are you okay?"

"Yes, I've accepted it. I've had over a month to think this all through and truth be told, I didn't want Darius to be the father, but he is."

"Keisha, I'm so sorry. I am so, so sorry."

"Man, there's never a dull moment with you, is there?" Jamel asked.

He was disappointed in his friend. Had he not slept with Stephanie, he wouldn't be sitting there trying to explain how he'd fathered a child he didn't anticipate on having.

"I'm sorry man. I didn't mean it like that. I'm just shocked. That's all."

"No apology necessary. I deserved it."

"How did you find out?"

"Stephanie's boyfriend showed up on our doorstep with

her. He came up from Atlanta to tell me. He had already been ruled out as her father, but he knew about the night Stephanie and I spent together. He knew about her obsession, and obviously put two and two together."

"So, he tracked you down? Who's been taking care of her since Stephanie's death?"

"He has. He's been raising her by himself, apparently."

"Wow. He sounds like a stand-up guy."

"Yes, he seems to love her like she was his own. He actually said if Darius wasn't the father that he was going to stop looking and continue to raise her."

"Isn't that something. So, what's going to happen now?"

"Well, she's eventually going to move here with us," said Keisha.

"We figured we would transition her here slowly because we don't want to disrupt her life so abruptly," Darius explained. "Man, do you need something to drink?"

"I could use a shot right about now, but I haven't had anything to drink since that first Sunday we went to church together."

"Believe it or not, that's the day we found out about Daria. They were waiting here when we got home."

"It's a good thing you were all prayed up and had the spirit of the Lord all over you," Monica laughed.

"You got that right. It's a good thing!"

"Well, we wanted you to know. I know this is all so sudden, but I wanted to make sure that if anything happens to us; both girls will be taken care of. I know it's asking a lot, but Daria is going to need godparents too," Darius admitted.

"Darius, you're right. It is a lot. Imagine having to tell that little girl when she gets older that I'm the one who killed her mother. How is that going to go over?"

"Monica, we'll have to cross that bridge when we get to it. Stephanie was insane. She was trying to kill Keisha. You did what you had to do."

"Yeah, I know but I can't help but think about the fact that I changed the course of that little girl's life by taking her mother away from her."

"But you had no idea. Knowing her mental state, she would have stalked someone else. If not us, then someone. Monica, you're going to have to eventually let that go."

"And maybe one day I will, but it's not going to be easy now. I'm going to have to look at her and know what I did."

"Every time you think about what you did, remind yourself of what her mother did."

"I'm going to have to think about this one. You don't need an answer right now, do you?" she asked.

"No, it'll probably be a couple of months at least before she moves here. Maybe even longer."

"Keisha, I think I need that drink now."

The two friends headed into the kitchen to open a bottle of Moscato.

"I haven't been drinking either, but I need a small glass of this wine after this. Keisha, you're a better woman than I will ever be. You've been through so much with Darius. I admire your strength."

"I know, right? If you'd told me two years ago that I was going to go through this and take it like a woman, I would have called you a liar. Straight up."

"Keisha, just know that I have your back. I'm so sorry that you're having to deal with this. You guys haven't even been married that long and here comes more drama. You've been going through so much, and all because of a brief encounter with a psycho woman. I can't believe this. My mother always told me to be careful who you attach yourself to. I didn't know what she meant when I was a teenager, but I sure get it now."

"Yes, you're right. There's been a lot of drama because of Darius and Stephanie, but when I married him; I made a commitment to be there with him through everything. Things aren't always going to be good. I could've just as easily been the one bringing all the drama into the marriage."

"Girl, no you couldn't. You don't even have that in you. You've never been that type of person. That's why I'm so surprised that you're handling this so well. You don't deserve it."

"Monica, neither of us deserves this; but Darius is truly my soulmate. I believe God brought us together for a reason. Darius is just having to pay for some of the things he did. God knows how much I can handle."

"It looks like you're having to pay too. Don't you see that?"

"Yes, I see it; but his drama in this situation is also my drama. It's going to be okay, Monica. I promise. Trust me. Right now, the important one in all of this is that little girl who needs to know that she is loved despite the circumstances that brought her into this life. It's not her fault."

"Yeah, I guess when you put it like that. It's not her fault. She didn't deserve it either."

"Keisha, whatever you need me to do; I'm here for you. For you and Darius too, and Daria. You have really shown me the true meaning of unconditional love."

"No, Jamel showed you first. I'm just reinforcing it."

"Okay, yeah. You got me on that one. He definitely showed me first. He shows me every day."

The ladies headed back into the family room where Jamel and Darius were now both sitting on the sofa.

"You guys okay in here?"

"Yes, we're good. I was just telling Darius that I would help him paint one of the guestrooms to make it beautiful just like Keyana's room. Now you're going to have two little princesses in the house. Wow!"

"Yeah, Keisha. I guess we're going to have to go shopping for furniture very soon."

Monica grabbed her friend's hand to reassure her that she was in her corner. Just let me know when you want to go.

"Having a sister might be a good thing for Keyana. She'll always have someone to play with."

"Yeah, that's true. She seems so lonely sometimes. I'm looking forward to seeing how they interact with one another. The day Daria was here, I had just put Keyana down for a nap, so they didn't get to see each other."

"Have you told your parents yet?"

"Yes, we went to both houses yesterday to break the news. They seemed to take it okay, although I could tell Keisha's parents were a little disappointed in me. I'm sure this isn't the life they were anticipating for their daughter."

"Darius, they're okay. I spoke to them earlier today and they seem to be handling it a lot better than they were handling it last night. Although, I thought they were okay with it then. Mom was concerned. She just doesn't want me to put too much on myself, but God only puts on us what we can bear, right?"

"You got that right."

"Monica, we better get out of here. Darius, just let me know when you're ready to paint. I see a custom designed jungle gym in your future too. I'll start drafting out the plans as soon as you say the word. I guess that huge backyard will be put to good use. There's plenty of room out there for one."

"Thanks, man."

"Keisha, you know I love you. If you need me, you know where to find me. If you just want to talk, I'm here for you. Remember that."

Monica gave her friend a long hug before they headed out the door. If Keisha was okay with all of this, then so was she. Her best friend's happiness was all that mattered.

"We'll see you in church tomorrow, right?"

"Yes, save us a seat if you get there before us."

"Will do."

"Love you guys."

"We love you too."

21 NEVER STOP PRAYING

Keisha and Darius made it to church a few minutes ahead of Monica and Jamel. Keyana was attending church with her grandparents. She saved a seat on either side of them for the two of them. Keisha knew that she was going to have to pray often to get through this. Even though she felt like she could handle it, she also recognized that there might be moments when she would feel the pain of what was going on. She might get a little overwhelmed. She didn't want the tension or stress to take a toll on their marriage or on her physical health.

"Hey, are you doing okay this morning?" Monica asked as she took her seat next to Keisha.

"Good morning. Yes, I'm doing just fine."

"Where's the baby?"

"She's with Mom and Dad this morning. They wanted her to go to church with them."

"Well, that's good. You probably needed a little break with everything that's going on. Are you ready for our trip to Turks & Caicos? Just two more weeks and we'll be headed out of here."

"Yes, I'm readier than you could ever imagine. After we

get back, we'll be deciding when Daria will be coming. Needless to say, we need this vacation because I don't know when we'll be able to take another one."

"Girl, I'm sure you'll still be able to vacation whenever you want. Between the two sets of grandparents, you'll be fine."

"You're probably right. I might be over exaggerating a little right now."

The ladies ended their conversation just as the choir took the stage to sing the songs they'd prepared for today's service. The first song up was "Your Steps Are Ordered" by Fred Hammond. Keisha knew that the song was so appropriate for what they were going through. God already knew how this was all going to play out. He knew what was going to happen long before either of them knew there was a Daria.

Keisha stood to give God the praise he deserved. She could feel the spirit fill her body as her eyes filled with tears while she sang the words to the song. Monica placed her arm around her friend to console her. Even though she tried to act like her exterior was tough, Monica knew she was hurting inside. Who wouldn't be? Darius held her hand. He was hurting too. He had brought shame to his family. Even though the birth of Daria wasn't the result of infidelity in his marriage, he realized that it was going to be difficult to avoid questions from people in church, at work, or wherever they went. Two daughters that close in age would raise at least a few eyebrows.

The next song up was by Anthony Brown & Group Therapy, "Trust in You." The choir was really hitting Keisha in an emotional way with everything they sang that morning. She was in tears again.

"Lord, please let them sing something a little more upbeat," Monica prayed.

Praise and worship ended, and it was time for church announcements. Maybe there would be something in there to lighten the mood.

"You okay, Keisha?" Monica asked.

"Yes, I'm okay but I know I've cried off all of my

makeup."

"It's okay, girl. You're still beautiful. Even with mascara and eyeliner running down your cheeks," Monica smiled.

Darius didn't know what to say or do. He just held her hand and rubbed her shoulder every now and then throughout the service. He had really made a mess of things. No matter what Keisha said, he knew there would be moments like this. It was going to take time to work through the pain and the reality of what they were going through. He knew he had a good woman. There were a lot out there who wouldn't have stayed around this long, but Keisha was really his ride or die. She had weathered many storms with him since they'd gotten married. Darius knew that Daria would be a constant reminder of what he had with Stephanie, no matter how brief it was. He had a lot of work to do to reassure his wife that things would be okay, but how could he? He wasn't 100 percent certain himself. He knew he just needed to keep praying that God would see them through. God would be their rock and strength. The values that his parents instilled in him regarding doing the right thing and believing in the Lord were all that he needed. He had to just keep on praying.

22 CAN'T LET GO

Darius dialed Antonio's number. He wanted to check on Daria and to make sure she didn't need anything. The call went straight to voicemail. The last five calls he'd placed over the past two days had also gone to voicemail.

"What in the world is going on? I've called Antonio multiple times and he's not answering or returning any of my calls."

"Darius, remember; Antonio is going through something that has to be difficult for him too."

"Yeah, I suppose you're right. I'm still a little concerned, though."

"Text me his number. I'll try to contact him today while you're at work."

"Okay, babe. I appreciate that. I love you."

"I love you too, Darius. Have a good day."

"You too."

Darius held Keisha in a tight embrace before grabbing his briefcase and heading out the door. Today would be the first day she'd have to spend with her thoughts without him. He wanted her to be okay. He was so afraid that she would wake up one day and realize that she'd taken on more than she could handle and would leave him. He was going to have to do a lot to make sure that it didn't happen. He couldn't stand the thought of living without her or Keyana. It just couldn't go down like that.

After lunch, Keisha dialed Antonio's number. The phone rang several times before he answered.

"Hello?"

"Hi, Antonio. It's Keisha. How are you today?"

"Oh, hi Keisha. I'm doing okay, I suppose. You?"

"I'm hanging in there. Darius has been trying to get ahold of you. Is everything okay? How's Daria?"

"We're both fine. Yeah, I did get his messages, but I wasn't ready to talk to him just yet."

"What do you mean? What's going on?"

"Keisha, I'm having a hard time dealing with the fact that I'm going to have to let her go. This is so hard for me. The whole time Stephanie was pregnant, I couldn't stop thinking about becoming a father. It was the happiest time of my life. Although she was doing things that weren't healthy for the pregnancy . . . the baby."

"I know this has to be hard for you. Believe me when I say I'm having a little difficulty with it too, but I've been praying about it. Maybe you should too. I've actually been praying for all of us and asking God to see us through this."

"Keisha, you're a good woman. I'm still in shock at how you've been dealing with the news. I don't know anyone who would have handled it the way you've been handling it."

"Antonio, I truly believe that things happen for a reason. That's the only way that I'm able to get through it. I know that God has a purpose for all of this and we really have no control over any of it. So, what's your hesitation about talking to Darius?"

"Keisha, I'm so used to her being here with me, that it breaks my heart to think about her living someplace else. Part of me regrets even coming to Maryland to talk to Darius about it, but the other part of me knows it was the right thing to do."

"I know. You seem like a decent person and to come all the way up here to deliver news like that took a lot. It says a lot about your character. You know, Darius and I have already been talking about your involvement in Daria's life after she moves here. He wants you to still be as active in her life as you've already been. He wants you to be able to spend time with her. He said you could come up here when you have free time, and he even mentioned her spending time during the summers and school breaks when she's old enough. What do you think about that?"

"He'd be willing to do that?"

"Of course, he would. Darius really is a good guy. He recognizes the fact that you've been the only father she's known since she was born. No one wants to disrupt her life in a way that could be emotionally damaging to her. I was even thinking about having her come here to spend time with us while living in Atlanta at least for a while before she moves here permanently. Darius and I haven't discussed that part yet, but it could work."

"Yeah, I could see something like that making it a little easier on all of us. It would give her time to get used to being around all of you while giving her time to get used to not being with me as much. Man, this hurts!"

"Yes, it does. I'll tell you what. I'll talk to Darius tonight about our discussion to see if he's up for letting her visit with us a few times over the next six months or so. To make the move easier. Is that okay?"

"Yeah, I can agree to that. I think that could work. Keisha, thank you for being such a warm-spirited person. This would have been even harder for me if I didn't feel that. I know she's going to be okay there."

"Thanks, Antonio. Your words mean a lot. She's been blessed to have someone like you in her life. Think about how many men would have been ready to get rid of her as soon as they found out there was no blood relation."

"I guess you're right. Keisha, thanks again. I better get going. Tell Darius I'm sorry for not calling him back. I'll be in touch soon."

"Okay. Maybe you could call him in a couple of days. It'll give me time to approach the plan with him."

"Sounds good. Have a good day, Keisha."

"And you as well, Antonio."

Keisha sat on the sofa with the phone still in her hand. Antonio was a good guy and she really thought bonding the relationship between the two men would be beneficial to the relationship that he would have with his daughter. They were going to have to find a way to be close friends. Almost as close as brothers for this to work. They were going to have to take a trip to Atlanta to see Daria and Antonio in their own environment. Darius needed to see how they were living. Then he might be in a better position to decide when she should be moved to Maryland.

Monica picked up the phone on the second ring. Keisha knew she worked from home on Mondays and Fridays.

"Hey, Keisha. What's up?"

"Hey. Not much. Just sitting over here thinking."

"You okay?"

"Yes, I am. I just got off the phone with Antonio. He's been dodging Darius's calls for the past few days, so I told him I'd try to reach out to him."

"And?"

"Girl, he's having a hard time with all of this. He doesn't want to let Daria go."

"Can you blame him? To him, she's his daughter. He's been taking care of her since she was born and after Stephanie's death, he's been playing the single dad role. I wish Darius had never met that chick. Look at everything that has happened because of meeting her. She tried to disrupt your marriage, steal your baby and kill you; and take your husband. Wow! That's so much. There are probably some more things that we don't even know about. She forced me to have to take her life. Do I need to go on?"

"No, I get your point. I get it more than you know, but we can't turn back time to change any of it. It has happened and now we have to deal with it."

"So how are you two going to get her away from him?"

"He'll let her go. It's just going to be tough. We talked about having a few visits with her. Maybe we could go down to Atlanta to visit them a couple of times. Then she could come up here to stay with us for a week or two. We could try that for a while before determining when she should move. Thank God, he's a good guy. Imagine how much more difficult it would be knowing that she was living with someone who didn't take good care of her. Someone who possibly abused her or something like that. She seems to be well taken care of. I don't think she wants for anything. Nothing at all."

"Yeah, that sounds like a good plan. It will also disrupt your life a little less than having her come here immediately. You have to remember Keyana in this whole equation too. She's been the only baby in the house and having another one around could be a little confusing for a minute."

"You know, I've thought about that. Luckily, she's still young. Once she gets over the fact that there'll be another baby in the house vying for attention, she'll be okay. I think she'll like having someone to play with."

"Either that, or she'll hate it," Monica laughed. "She's going to have to learn to share her toys and her parents. That's a lot for a child."

"You're right, but she's a good girl. She'll be okay. We'll just have to give her some time. That's all."

"I hear you. Keisha, I just don't want you to take those rose-colored glasses off and realize that this is too much."

"Monica, I'm thinking about this from all angles. I recognize what could happen, but I'm trying to keep an open mind about it all. Trying to think about it as positively as I can. I've even thought about us going to some sort of family counseling. I don't think we need it right now, but I'm sure there might come a time when we do."

"Girl, you might not think you need it right now, but you just might want to be proactive and get a couple of sessions in before you start interacting more with Daria. It could be good for you, Darius, and her."

"You might be right. Anyway, I better let you go. I forgot you're on the clock."

"Okay, lady. I love you. If you need me, just call. I'll always be here for you. You know that, right?"

"Yes, I do. Love you too, girl."

Keisha knew that Monica's intentions were good. She just didn't want to see her get hurt any more than she already had. Her parents were sort of responding in the same way. They loved Darius just like he was their own son, but he had really created a mess that they were all going to have to clean up. Yet, she also loved and respected her husband. If she could hold on to the love and respect, she knew she would be able to see him through whatever trials they had to go through. After all, you can't change your past. All you can do is make sure not to continue to make the same mistakes. Unfortunately, Antonio and Keisha were both innocent victims in all of this. Keisha was going to have to figure out how to let Daria into her heart where a daughter belonged, and Antonio was going to have to figure out how to let go, at least a little. She hoped they would both get there in due time.

23 VACATION

The group arrived at JAGS McCartney International Airport in the Grand Turk Islands a few minutes ahead of schedule. Monica looped her arm through Keisha's after they exited the airplane.

"You ready for some much-needed relaxation and fun?"

"Monica, you have no idea how ready I am for this. I think we all could use a break away from the reality we left back in PG County, right?"

"Yes. Can we agree not to think about any of it while we're out here?"

"You've got a deal. Of course, I'll have to check on Keyana. You do realize that, right?"

"Girl, I'm not talking about Keyana. I'm talking about everything else. So, let's inhale and exhale and leave it where it is. Ready?"

Keisha did as Monica instructed. She took a deep breath, held it for a few seconds and then released it.

"See? Doesn't that feel better already?"

"Yeah, it actually does."

Darius and Jamel headed toward the baggage claim area to retrieve their luggage from the carousel.

"Man, how many bags did you bring?" Darius asked Jamel as he watched him load six Louis Vuitton suitcases onto the cart.

"You know Monica. I think Keisha's been rubbing off on her. I don't know why you're looking at all our bags. I'm sure Keisha brought just as many. You're not fooling me."

"Yeah, you're right. I think she has three or four herself. I just brought two. I just need some shorts and t-shirts, swimming trunks, and what I need to wear for the dinner on Saturday. I did throw in another suit just in case there was some other event we were going to attend that I hadn't been made aware of. You know how the ladies are. They didn't come all the way out here to just swim in the clear blue ocean, right?"

"You got that right. I brought another suit too just in case."

"Man, this ten-day vacation is definitely what I need right now. Both of us."

"Yeah, it couldn't have come at a better time, considering everything. I'm glad you guys are here with us."

"We wouldn't have missed it."

"So, Monica still has no idea that you brought her all the way out here to ask her to marry you, huh?"

"No, she has no idea. I'm glad the two of us have talked about our future together because initially, I wanted to get married on the island. It wasn't until she started talking about getting married in the church that I knew we would just be getting engaged out here. She'll have time to plan our wedding back in Maryland once we get home. I'm going to let her decide on the date.

"That's the way it was supposed to be for us too, man. Until we found out we were having a baby. The plan changed quickly, but I was thinking about renewing our vows on our fifth anniversary in the church. The way it should have been the first time. Keisha doesn't know it yet, but I'm sure she would love that. Besides, after everything we've been going through, we'll need a vow renewal by then."

"Knowing her like I do, I agree. She would love that."

After loading all the luggage onto two carts, the men headed toward the ladies before exiting the airport for the limo.

"Wow! A limo from the airport, huh? Jamel, you're too fancy for me."

"Keisha, you haven't seen anything yet. We're going to have the most amazing time ever. Trust me."

"I believe it. Thanks again for inviting us."

"Isn't this beautiful?" Monica gazed out of the limo window at the beautiful palm trees lining the winding road. The ocean was just a stone's throw away. "I can't wait to see the hotel we're staying at."

The limo pulled into the driveway of a beautiful hotel. It seemed to not have many rooms, which was good. It meant optimal privacy. The couples could enjoy more privacy with just a few families nearby. You couldn't ask for anything better than that.

The chauffeur removed all the suitcases from the trunk of the limo and the two that occupied the front passenger seat. Jamel walked up to the front door of the hotel and instead of opening it, he inserted a key into the keyhole.

"Jamel, what are you doing?" Monica asked.

"I'm opening the door, so we can go in. What do you mean?"

"Wait a minute. Isn't this a hotel?"

"No, it's our accommodations for the next ten days."

"The whole thing?"

"Yes, all 20,500 square feet. Our suite is on the first floor. Keisha and Darius, you can pick from any of the other four. There's one more on the first floor and three on the second level. All of them have one or two king sized beds and master bathrooms. If you want to stay in one room tonight to try it out and pick another one tomorrow; it's up to you."

"Man, you have got to be kidding me. You rented this whole place?"

"I sure did. We have a fully equipped kitchen, indoor and

outdoor pools, jacuzzi; you name it. I hired a chef to prepare all our meals and there will be maid service twice a day. There's also a washer and dryer. I couldn't tell you any of this because it would have ruined the surprise. Although it might have meant that Monica wouldn't have brought so many bags," Jamel laughed.

"No, Jamel. She would have still brought as many bags. You've created a monster, you know that don't you?" Keisha joked.

"It's okay. We can use one of the extra rooms to stage the luggage if you like. I want you guys to be as comfortable as possible. If the bags are out of sight, I believe we'll have a better time."

"I agree with that. Thanks, man."

Jamel handed the limo driver who had just carried the last of the bags into the house, a $100 tip. The limo driver handed him his business card before heading down the u-shaped driveway.

"Well, let's get these bags to their resting place so that I can show you all around the house."

Keisha and Darius opted for the third bedroom on the second floor because the bathroom was equipped with a soaking tub with jets and a separate shower that was big enough to have a party in. It could fit ten people, easy. The French doors led out to a huge balcony that overlooked the ocean. You could walk down a spiral staircase and follow a sandy path right down to the beach.

"This is incredible! Jamel really outdid himself, didn't he?"

"He sure did, babe." Darius held Keisha from behind as they took in the beautiful scenery. He knew they had two days before the big event. "Let's go meet up with those two so that Jamel can give us the grand tour. This is something else."

"Yes, it is. Okay, let me use the bathroom first and I'll be right out."

Darius pulled the small box from the jewelry store out of his carry-on bag and waited for Keisha to come out of the bathroom.

"Babe, I have something for you. I know it can't fix what's going on right now in our lives, but I wanted to let you know how much I love and appreciate you."

He handed her the box. Keisha looked at it for a few seconds before opening it. Inside, she found a beautiful diamond ring with two intertwined hearts surrounded by diamonds. She looked at Darius as lovingly as she could. He still had her heart and always would.

"These are our hearts, babe. They're connected, and no man or woman can separate that."

"You're right, babe. Thank you so much. It's beautiful."

Darius took the three-carat ring out of the box and placed it on Keisha's right ring finger. He took her hand and kissed it.

"I love you more than you could ever imagine. More than love, remember that."

"I love you too." Keisha stood on her toes to kiss him.

There was something different about this kiss. She really did love him and had his back in ways that some wouldn't understand. Keisha honored the vow she took and always would. No one could come between them. No one. Hand in hand, they headed downstairs to meet up with Monica and Jamel. This was going to be some vacation.

24 TAKING IN THE SCENERY

After the grand tour of the property and the delicious lunch prepared by Chef Jacques, the two couples decided to relax on the beach. Keisha had bought a beautiful fuchsia two-piece bikini at Nordstrom's a few weeks prior in anticipation of the trip. She had actually bought three new bikinis and a new one-piece suit. Even though she had given birth to Keyana, you couldn't tell. There wasn't an inch of fat or a stretch mark in sight. She was Darius's show stopper and always would be.

"Keisha, I'm loving those highlights in your hair. When the sun hits them, they look incredible."

"Thanks, Monica. I figured it would be a good look for the trip. Yours looks beautiful too."

"Thanks, girl."

The ladies waded in waist deep water, trying not to get their hair wet on the first day of the trip. Maybe later in the week, but not now. It was too soon to have to spend too much time fooling around with it. Right now, they just wanted to relax and enjoy the sun and the beach.

The guys came back with two jet skis.

"Get on! Let's take these things for a few spins around the beach!"

Keisha jumped onto the back of the jet ski Darius was on while Monica climbed on behind Jamel.

"Remember the jet skis while we were in St. Thomas? We had so much fun!"

"Yeah, we did; but you definitely did. It became clear during the jet ski ride that you and Jamel had a thing going on. At least as far as Shawn could tell!" Keisha yelled over the roar of the engines.

Jamel and Darius took off on the jet skis with their ladies holding on tightly. They rode around the perimeter of the beach before heading out into deeper water. Keisha could see some of the fish scurrying to get away from the jet skis. She even spotted what she thought to be a barracuda and made a mental note to leave her jewelry in the safe in the closet the next time they came out for a swim. She knew that barracudas were attracted to shiny things and didn't want to put herself in the line of one of them just because of all her bling.

After an hour, the fellas drove the ladies back to shallow water so that they could disembark.

"We'll meet you on the beach after we return them!" Jamel yelled over the roar of the engines.

"We'll be right here!"

After finding a comfortable spot on the beach, they moved four lounge chairs next to each other under a big cabana that would shield them from the sun. It was too early for sunburn. They were just getting here and wanted to enjoy every moment without things like puffy hair and sunburn.

"Monica, Jamel outdid himself on this trip. I knew it would be big, but I had no idea to what extent."

"Yeah, he's something else; isn't he? If someone had told me years ago that the two of us would end up here, I wouldn't have believed it. I never thought I was worthy of such treatment. Jamel has shown me just how important I am. He's constantly telling me how beautiful I am and how special I am to him. I hear the words I love you every day. No one has ever treated me like this. Sometimes, I have to pinch myself because I still have a hard time believing that it's happening to me."

"Monica, I have always known that you were worthy of being treated just like this. I'm just glad that you can see it for yourself now. You have an amazing man and I pray that you two have years on top of years of bliss. Even when you're old and grey with grandchildren, and even great-grands."

"Thank you, Keisha. You have always been in my corner and I love you for it. When I was making bad decisions, you never abandoned me. You've always been a true friend and I couldn't imagine not having what we have."

With her hands over her eyes blocking the sun, Monica could see Jamel and Darius coming up the beach. She smiled when she envisioned being in a park with her own babies, then years and years into the future; she could see her and Jamel playing with their grandchildren. Life was so good.

As the men got closer, Monica jumped up from her lounge chair and ran toward Jamel. She jumped into his arms and wrapped her legs around his waist. Keisha met Darius with a warm hug and a huge kiss. She wanted to stay in the moment. No fears, no worries. Nothing but love from her husband and her best friends. They gathered their belongings from the cabana and headed up the path back to the villa to get ready for a nice romantic private dinner for four. Chef Jacques was working on quite a spread at Jamel's request. He had also hired a steel drum band to play Calypso style music while they dined. After dinner, they would enjoy some dancing. It was going to be a wonderful evening. One they would not soon forget. In fact, Jamel wanted to make sure that they wouldn't forget any part of this trip. It would be the topic of conversation for years to come. That's what he was aiming for. Something at least, Monica would always remember.

25 SETTING THE MOOD

Keisha stood in the closet trying to decide between the turquoise halter maxi dress or the peach two-piece skirt set that showed all her curves. The top exposed her stomach and back while the waistband of the skirt fell at the edge of her hips and cascaded down to the floor. There was a split that came up the front left leg exposing her skin from the ankle up to her mid-thigh. Darius knew she would look amazing in either, even though he'd never seen the outfits before. They were a part of the vacation wardrobe she'd purchased just for the trip.

"I think I'm going to go with the turquoise one for tonight. I'll wear the other one tomorrow night."

"Yes, I agree," Darius smiled knowing that the peach outfit would be beautiful for the engagement dinner that next evening.

He already knew that Jamel had planned something very special for them. He also knew that Monica's parents would be flying in early the following afternoon along with Jamel's mom and dad. Darius knew there were things to be learned from watching Jamel and how he wined and dined his woman. He was quite the romantic.

Darius and Keisha took a long, warm shower together in

the space that looked like it was designed for a shower party. He lathered her back with soap that smelled like fresh coconut and pineapples, then held her closely.

"Keisha, I love you so much. I could stay here forever."

"Yes, I could too. This place is amazing."

Turning to face him, Keisha looked into her husband's eyes. She then planted kisses on his chest before resting her cheek against him. Darius gently kissed the crease in her neck before lifting her into his arms. They shared intimate moments in that place until the water began to run cold. There was always so much passion between them. After the encounter was over, they quickly soaped each other down and rinsed off in the cold water before heading into the bedroom.

"Wow! I sure hope we didn't use all the hot water before Jamel and Monica could shower."

"Me too."

Darius poured lotion into his right hand and smeared it with his left. He rubbed the mixture onto Keisha's back and down both of her legs.

"Thanks, babe."

"You're welcome. Come here, I'll help you step into that dress."

After securing her strapless bra in the back, Darius held her arm to maintain her balance while she stepped into the dress. It was as beautiful as the turquoise sea.

"This color looks beautiful on you."

"Thanks. What are you wearing?"

Darius held up the linen suit that he'd worn when they got married.

"Good choice," Keisha smiled while reminiscing about the day she walked down onto the beach to meet her king.

"I bought something new for our dinner tomorrow night and figured this one would be sufficient for tonight."

"Babe, you'd look good in a pair of swimming trunks and flip flops if that's what you wanted to wear."

They both laughed. We'd better get going. Jamel said dinner would start promptly at 7:00 P.M. It's 6:45 right now.

"I'm ready, my love. Let's go."

As Darius opened the bedroom door, they could hear the steel drum band playing downstairs.

"What in the world? Is that a band?"

"Yes, your boy went all out for this dinner. He hired a steel drum band to perform while we ate. I believe he said they would be with us for three hours. Maybe even four."

"Talk about setting the mood!"

Keisha began to dance as she reached the bottom of the long staircase. Monica walked over and began to dance with her. Both ladies looked amazing! Monica wore a hot pink off the shoulder maxi dress. Her hair was pinned up in the back and beautiful curls cascaded down either side of her face.

"You look beautiful, my friend."

"So, do you, Keisha."

The two ladies hugged before heading in the direction of the dining area. The food looked delicious. They were having lobster, grilled fish, grilled corn, tropical fruit, some sort of pasta salad, potatoes, and steamed asparagus. Chef Jacques entered the dining area carrying a platter of filet mignon that would also be a part of the meal.

"Wow, Jamel. What are we going to do with all of this?"

"Eat up. I want you guys to enjoy yourselves. What we don't eat today, we can indulge in for lunch tomorrow unless you guys want something else. There are a bunch of college students renting out the villa next door. I'm sure they wouldn't mind helping us finish some of this food. I'll have Chef Jacques load up some of it and take it over on his way out. He said he knows the family of one of the kids."

"Yeah, you might have to do that. This is way too much, man."

"Nothing is too good for you guys. Have a seat."

Jamel pulled out Monica's chair for her to take a seat next to him.

"Monica, you look so beautiful."

She blushed as she gathered her dress before sitting down.

"Thanks, baby. You look great too."

Jamel blessed the food before the meal was served. He had also hired two servers, so they wouldn't have to lift a finger.

Monica looked around the candlelit room. She still couldn't figure out what she did to deserve all of this. Remembering what Keisha had said earlier that day, she wondered, why not her? She was worthy of this treatment and hoped to have the rest of her life to enjoy it with Jamel.

The couples spent two hours following the dinner, dancing to the music of the island. It was a good way to burn off the calories they'd just taken in. The day had been one right out of a fairytale and Keisha couldn't wait to see what Jamel had in store for them tomorrow.

"How can Jamel top this day? I haven't had this much fun in a long time."

"Don't worry babe. I have a feeling each day will be better than the one before. He's trying to show his woman a good time. We just happen to be along for the ride."

"Yes, but I'm having such a good time too. I'm so glad we came."

"There was no way we were going to miss this. Trust me."

26 EASE YOUR TROUBLED MIND

Keisha awoke to the sound of Chef Jacques preparing breakfast downstairs. She inhaled the scent of turkey bacon, steak, sautéed peppers and onions, and some sort of egg dish

"Omelets," she mumbled.

"What'd you say, babe?" Darius snuggled up close behind her.

"I smell breakfast. What time is it?"

Darius reached for the clock on the nightstand holding it at a distance to gain his focus.

"It's 7:15."

"I guess we'd better get showered. He's probably serving at 8:00."

"Come here."

He grabbed her around the waist and pulled her closer to plant three kisses down her back. Keisha wiggled herself free before turning to face him.

"Can I get a little dessert before breakfast?"

"I suppose that would be okay. Just don't ruin your appetite."

"I could stay in this bed all day with you. I wouldn't even need breakfast."

Keisha felt warm inside when she looked into his eyes.

Despite everything, with each day, her love for him grew. She loved him more today than she did the day before and nothing or no one could change that. She leaned in to kiss him.

"I love you, Darius. More than you could ever know."

"Babe, I do know. I love you too. I am so thankful to have you. I've taken you through so much, and you still love me."

"It's unconditional, babe. I learned that from you."

Keisha straddled Darius. Placing both palms on either side of his chest, she began to massage the tension away. He closed his eyes and enjoyed the moment. She hadn't given him a massage in a while.

"Turn over."

Darius lifted her up and placed her on his side so that he could follow the command. He noticed she was a little lighter than she usually was. Perhaps she was a little stressed, although she would never admit it. Her appetite appeared to be normal, but Keisha had a way of keeping things in. He knew life had handed them a lot, but he thought they were managing to get through without too much emotional stress.

"Baby, are you really okay?"

"What do you mean?"

"We haven't had a lot of time to talk through all of this. I mean, we've talked about how we thought it should play out; but you've never expressed how you really feel about all of it."

"Honey, I told you I was okay. The bottom line is that it happened, and we must deal with it. There's no point in dwelling on what happened in the past, babe. I'm really okay. Besides, we're on vacation, so let's not talk about it."

She bent over to kiss the side of his face.

"Now, I thought you wanted your dessert."

Darius turned over again to touch his wife in ways that had become so familiar, but never boring. He could touch her a million times with as much excitement as the first time. They made love to the sounds of the ocean crashing against the shoreline and the soft whisper of the wind whirling through the room. Keisha loved sleeping with the patio doors open whenever there was an ocean nearby. There was something serene about it. The ocean had a way of relaxing even the most troubled mind. She left all their concerns back in Maryland and she wanted to enjoy the days with her husband and her best friends. Nothing else mattered. She knew Keyana and Daria were both fine in the care of her parents and Antonio respectively. Now, if she could only get Darius to not only stop thinking about the most recent drama but to stop talking about it at least until they returned home.

"Babe, are you coming?" Keisha yelled from the shower.

"I'm right here."

Darius stared at her through the glass. She was as beautiful as ever. He knew he was blessed to have her and would do everything within his power to make sure that she didn't have to endure any more issues because of him. After he stepped in, the two caressed under the stream of warm water like it would wash away all their troubles. At least for now.

"How about we go for a swim after breakfast?"

"Yes, that sounds good to me. I guess we better find out if Jamel has already made plans for us."

"No, there's nothing going on until later this evening."

"Oh yeah? What's that?"

"Nothing, just dinner. That's all. I talked to him last night after you fell asleep. He said Monica wanted to lie on the beach for a while and there was something about taking her shopping at noon. I figured we could swim for a while, shower, and change and then join them for shopping. He asked if we wanted to come."

Darius was trying to make sure that Keisha was still in the dark about the engagement dinner. In no way did he want Monica to find out about it before this evening.

"Shopping? Yeah, that sounds like a lot of fun to me. I'm in."

Keisha slid into the emerald green one-piece bathing suit she'd recently purchased. It went beautifully with the emerald green, hot pink, and royal blue skirt that fell just above the knee and her green flip-flops.

"Babe, I bought these swimming trunks for you."

"I see," Darius smiled and stepped into the emerald green swimming trunks. "You're funny."

"What?"

"Remember that clothing brand that was out when we were kids? Garanimals or something like that? If there was a tiger on the tag of a shirt and one on the tag of a pair of pants or shorts, you knew the items would match?"

"Yes, I remember. What are you trying to say?"

"I mean, look at our outfits. We look like we've been shopping at the Garanimals store."

"Stop playing, Darius."

I'm just kidding. I'm proud to let everyone know that we're together.

"You wait until you see what I picked out for you for tonight."

"What?"

"I'm just kidding. Oh, and for the record. Garanimals are still around. I ordered some things from their website for Keyana when she was a newborn. Some cute little onesies and skeggings."

"Keisha, what is a skegging?"

"It's a skirt with leggings under it."

"Oh, is that what it's called?"

"Yes, it is."

Darius erupted into laughter as they headed downstairs.

"Wow, you learn something new every day. You'll have to find her some more of those. She looks so cute in them."

"I'm going to buy some for both of them as soon as we get back home."

He grabbed her hand as they walked through the foyer and into the kitchen area.

"Well, it's about time you two decided to join us," said Jamel.

"Man, it's not my fault that you and your lady have taken an oath of celibacy. We're married, so it takes us a little longer to get ready if you know what I mean."

"Darius, you can spare us the details with your nasty self," Monica shook her head as if what he'd said was the most disgusting thing. "Good morning, Keisha."

"Hey, lady. Don't mind him."

One of the servers from the night before poured orange juice into Darius and Keisha's glasses.

"Would you like a cup of coffee, Miss?" asked Simone, the server.

"Yes, Simone; as a matter of fact, I would love a cup. Darius, you want some?"

"No, none for me. The orange juice and a glass of ice water will be fine."

Simone returned with two glasses of ice water on a tray with a small pot of coffee, sweetener, and creamer.

"What will you be eating today?"

"I think I'll have an egg white omelet with peppers, tomatoes, spinach, mushrooms, and a little cheddar cheese. I smelled turkey bacon earlier. If I could also get a couple slices of that and a slice of wheat toast."

"Sir, what would you like?"

"First, please call me Darius," he hesitated. "I'd like a steak, medium well with an omelet just like the one Keisha just ordered. I would love to have a croissant with mine, though."

"Okay, I'll be back shortly with your orders."

Chef Jacques had already prepared the food which was now being kept warm in sterling silver serving platters, but the omelets were being made to order. The chef was standing out on the balcony talking to someone on his cell phone when Simone gestured for him to come inside.

"So, what time are we headed out into town?"

"I was thinking about 1:30 or 2:00," Jamel took a long sip from his orange juice glass. "Monica wants to pick up some souvenirs. I figured we could go swimming or snorkeling if you guys want to. Keisha, you couldn't go when we were in St. Thomas because you were pregnant. It should be fun."

"You can blame it on the pregnancy if you want to. I'm not sure I want to be that close to fish that big."

"Come on babe. It'll be fun. Just try it for a few minutes and if you don't like it we can stop."

"Okay, you know what? I'm with Keisha. I'm really not trying to get my hair wet just yet," Monica ran her fingers through her beautiful curls that had been holding up quite nicely so far.

"You know something, Monica's right. Let's save snorkeling for another day."

Jamel didn't want her hair to be in disarray for the surprise this evening. So, snorkeling was out.

"I think we should just enjoy the water and take in a little sun. Maybe we can rent a kayak. That should be better if no one falls out, no wet hair," he laughed. "All jokes aside. I figured we could shop for a few hours this afternoon and grab a snack or light lunch while we're out because we're having a late dinner tonight."

"Well, that gives us plenty of time to enjoy the beach. I'm ready!" Monica stood from the table. "Let me grab my bag from the room. I'll be right back."

"Keisha, I need you to keep her distracted while we're out later. If you could convince her that you need to check out something in a store away from where Darius and I will be, that would help. There's something I want to buy for her and I don't want her to see it until tonight."

"Oh, okay. I can do that, she said after swallowing the last bite of her omelet."

After Monica returned to the kitchen, they headed out the patio doors and down to the beach. It was already turning out to be another beautiful day.

27 WHAT TIME IS IT?

Keisha and Monica headed into a boutique in the Regent Village to try on a dress that Keisha spotted from the storefront window.

"Isn't this beautiful?"

"Yes, it sure is. It looks like it was made for you, but I think you need to go one size down."

Monica walked back to the rack to grab a size six.

"Keisha has lost some weight," she thought, as she walked back toward the dressing room. "Considering all she's been going through, I'm not surprised," Monica said in a whisper.

"Here you go, Keisha."

Monica stood on her toes and handed the dress still on its hanger over the dressing room door.

"Thanks."

Keisha slid the size six dress over her head and adjusted it. She turned to the left to admire her image in the mirror. Then to the right, as she opened the dressing room door so that Monica could give her opinion on the item that she would soon own.

"What do you think?"

"Girl, that dress looks so good on you!"

Keisha stood outside of the dressing room in front of the mirrored wall. The dress caressed her body in all the right places. She knew Darius would love it.

"You know those Christian Louboutin shoes Darius bought last month? The ones with the straps that wrap around the ankle a couple of times?"

"Yes, I remember. You're right. Those are the shoes for this dress. So, this one's a keeper then, right?"

"It sure is."

Keisha glanced at her watch. The men were supposed to meet them at the boutique after Jamel bought Monica's gift.

"You know something? There's another one out there that I think you should try. Come here, let me show you."

Keisha walked up to a rack that had some beautiful pieces by Diane Von Furstenberg. She grabbed a wrap dress that tied at the waist.

"If you don't try this dress on, I'm going to. I think it's really nice. Look at the colors."

"Yeah, it's very pretty. Do you think Jamel would like it?"

"Monica, Jamel would love this on you."

She grabbed an eight and a ten from the rack and headed toward the dressing room.

"You better start with the eight, because I think the ten might be too big."

Monica agreed and took the size eight from its hanger. After stepping out of her sundress, she stuck her arms into the sleeve openings and wrapped the dress around her waist, securing it by the two strands of material reserved to ensure that it stayed closed.

"Wow! You were right. The eight is perfect!"

Monica came out of the dressing room so that Keisha could give the dress her stamp of approval.

"You like it?"

"Yes, I love, love, love it!"

"I'm probably going to have to find a pair of shoes to go with it, though."

"You'll find some. If not, I know I have a pair that would

look good with it. You know you can always borrow them if you need to."

"Okay. It's settled then. I'm getting this one."

After Monica put her sundress back on, they headed toward the register to pay for their items. In an hour and a half, together they had spent over $1,100 on two dresses. Luckily, Darius and Jamel walked in as the sales associate was putting Monica's dress in a hanging bag.

"Perfect timing," Keisha remarked. "Any longer and we would have racked up quite the bill."

"Did you find something beautiful, babe?"

"I sure did. You're going to love it, isn't he Monica?"

"Yep. What did you guys get?"

"Oh, just a couple of souvenirs," said Jamel as he held up a bag from one of the souvenir shops. "You guys want to go to any other stores?"

"No, I think we're good," said Monica.

They walked through town stopping in a few more stores before grabbing a light bite to eat at one of the cafes.

"We're having a special dinner tonight, so don't ruin your appetites, please," Jamel insisted.

"More special than last night?" Keisha asked.

"Yes, more special than last night."

"What's the occasion?"

"Keisha, look around. Do we really need one?"

"No, I guess you're right."

"What time is it?" Jamel glanced at his watch. "Wow, we'd better head back. Dinner will be served at sundown and we still have to get showered and changed."

They headed back in the direction of the villa when the limo driver who brought them from the airport pulled up. Only this time, he was driving a Cadillac SUV.

"Wow, are we glad to see you!"

Keisha climbed into the backseat and slid to the left so that the others could get in.

They were back at the villa in twenty minutes. Jamel handed the driver $50 before exiting.

"You guys go ahead in. I have to talk to Henry for a second."

"Hey, man. Did you get the parents here safely?"

"Yes, sir. They're already inside. They've been given the instructions that you told me to give them. Neither of them will make a sound. While the four of you are getting ready, they're going to take their places near the villa that has been set up for the event. The flowers have all been delivered and everything is all set. The only thing left to do would be to light the candles and Simone and Sarai will be taking care of that just before you guys come out."

"Thanks, man. I really appreciate you."

"Not a problem, Jamel. Your father and I go back so far, we're like brothers. We all want what's best for you and this evening is going to go off without a hitch."

"I sure hope so."

"You can tell me all about it tomorrow over lunch. Your father asked me to join you all. I hope that's okay."

"It sure is. We'll see you then."

28 THE PROPOSAL

Jamel handed Darius his bag from the jewelry store that was hidden inside the bag from the souvenir shop.

"Thanks, man. I'm not going to give this to Keisha until we get back home. This trip is all about Monica. When are you going to give it to her?"

"I've got it all planned. I'm going to give it to her just before I ask her to marry me. While she's focusing on the watch, I'll be getting down on my knee to ask for her hand. When she sees our parents, she'll be thinking that a proposal must be coming. The watch is to throw her off."

"Jamel, you're clever."

"I'm a little nervous, believe it or not. I've never asked anyone to marry me before. I want this to be perfect. I love her so much, man."

"I know you do. Whenever you're with her, it's all over your face. You wear the love you have for her all over you."

"Well, we'll see how this thing plays out in a couple of hours. Our parents are tucked away in their suites. They're going to make their way out to the beach while we're getting ready. She has no idea that they're here. I bought her a beautiful red dress to wear. She doesn't even know about that yet. I'm going to lay it out while she's in the shower."

"You weren't kidding when you said this whole thing was a surprise, huh?"

"No, I wasn't kidding at all."

"Well, I'm going to head upstairs to start getting ready. God bless you, man."

"Thanks, Darius; but God has already blessed me so much. He just keeps on doing it."

Darius smiled at his best friend and headed up the stairs to his bride. He couldn't believe how far they'd all come in such a short time, and although he and Keisha were going through some tribulations in their marriage; he believed that God would get them to the other side of it unscathed. In fact, he was certain that they would not have made it without him.

"Babe, you okay?"

"Yes, I'm in the bathroom. I just got out of the shower. I still need to get my outfit together for dinner. Do you need me to do anything while you bathe?"

"No, I'm fine," He grabbed Keisha around the waist and kissed her gently on her neck.

"I can't wait to see what's for dinner. I'm getting a little hungry."

"How are you feeling?"

"I feel great. In fact, better than I've felt in about a month or so."

Keisha stepped into her panties before putting on the matching bra.

"I spoke to Mom and Dad earlier to check on Keyana. They said she was doing good."

"Oh, okay. That's good to hear. I actually miss the little munchkin."

"So do I, but I am having a wonderful time out here. I could actually get used to this."

Darius knew she deserved the kind of life they were living right now. Thanks to Jamel, they were getting an opportunity to experience it. In the back of Darius's mind, he knew he was going to have to get better about showering his woman with the things in life that she deserved. After watching how Jamel was doing it, he realized that he was falling short. He could afford it. Well, maybe not quite on Jamel's level, but he wasn't far behind.

"Babe, I think we should start taking more vacations like this. What do you think?" The shower water cascaded down his back.

"Babe?"

"Hey, sorry. I was on the phone."

"Who were you talking to?"

"I was checking on Daria. Antonio said she's doing okay."

"Oh, okay. What made you decide to call him?"

"Well, I checked on Keyana. It's only right that I check on Daria too. We have to start treating her like she's a part of this family too, don't you agree?"

"Yes, you're absolutely right. Thanks, Babe."

"You don't have to thank me. You'd better hurry. It's almost time for dinner."

Keisha handed Darius his underwear and wife beater to rush him along.

"What's this? Aren't you always the last one to get ready? I can't believe you're already dressed. You must be pretty excited about this dinner," joked Darius.

"Actually, I am. I've been having so much fun, I can't wait to see what Jamel has planned for tonight."

"I'm sure it's going to be something," he smiled. "What do you think about a long walk on the beach after dinner?"

"That sounds very romantic. Yes, let's do it."

"Where's everybody? Are we early?"

"No, dinner is being served outside this evening. We're supposed to wait here for Jamel."

"What in the world? We're having dinner on the patio tonight, huh?"

"Yeah, something like that," Jamel kept conversation to a minimum. He didn't want to give anything away.

"Hey, lady," Monica said as she cascaded into the room with Jamel on her arm.

"Wow! You look absolutely beautiful!"

"Thanks. Jamel bought me this amazing dress. It's something, isn't it?" Monica twirled so Keisha could take in the dress from every angle.

It was a deep red strapless dress secured in the back by strings that crisscrossed from the small of Monica's back and up to her bra strap area. The strings were the only thing keeping it in place. She wore a beautiful diamond necklace with matching earrings. Another gift from Jamel. Monica looked like a million bucks.

"Wow! You do look beautiful." Darius kissed her on the cheek before hugging his best friend.

"Jamel, man. The surprises just keep coming and coming."

The four headed out the patio door and down the stairs leading to the beach.

"Jamel, where are we going?" Monica looked confusingly into his eyes.

"I've set up something out here for our dinner. I thought it would be different."

Monica smiled as she grasped his hand tightly in hers. The sound of a violin could be heard off in the distance. There were candles lining the walkway leading down to a pavilion just feet away from the shore. Huge floral arrangements lined the perimeter for the sake of privacy.

"This pavilion wasn't here earlier. Jamel, did you do this?"

"Of course, I did. I wanted tonight to be special."

"Babe, this whole trip has already been special, and it's only been two days."

Jamel pulled out a chair for Monica to take a seat. Darius followed suit.

Keisha reached her hand across the table to grab the hand of Monica who was beaming with excitement like a child on her birthday.

Keisha's eyes began to water when she saw shadows coming up from the beach.

"Something's about to go down," she said to herself.

Darius took his seat next to Keisha.

"Babe, I bought you something." Jamel handed her a box wrapped neatly in silver paper.

"Jamel, what have you done?" Monica asked as she tore the wrapping from the box.

"Is this what I think it is?"

"It's the only thing I could think of that I hadn't already bought you."

The face of the Rolex was surrounded by diamonds. It would make the perfect addition to the jewelry that Jamel had already bought her. Even the piece she had yet to find out about.

"Babe, it's beautiful!" She said. "Can you help me put it on?"

Jamel removed it from the box and fastened it securely on her tiny wrist. There's something inscribed on the inside. You'll have to read it later.

"Okay, thank you so much," she kissed him gently on his lips.

"Oh, I almost forgot. I have something else for you."

Jamel reached into the floral arrangement directly behind Monica's chair. Henry had been instructed to leave the ring box there. He gestured for the parents to enter the pavilion.

"Oh my God! Mom! Dad! What are you guys doing here?"

Monica was so excited that she hadn't noticed Jamel's parents moving in on her left side. She jumped from her chair and hugged them both tightly as the tears began to fall down both cheeks.

"Jamel, what are you doing?"

"Monica, the day we met; I knew there was something special about you although you hardly knew I existed. I watched you walk through life being treated in ways far outside of what you truly deserved. I wanted to protect you from anyone who was in your life to do you harm. Unfortunately, you had to go through some things that I couldn't protect you from; but still, I wanted to be your guardian angel. When we were in St. Thomas with Darius and Keisha, I knew that it was just a matter of time before we would get to this day. You have made me the happiest man walking the face of this earth and I cannot wait to be able to call you my fiancé – my wife." Jamel took a deep breath before continuing.

"Monica Andrea Stevens, you are the air I breathe, my rib . . . the woman God created for me, and; it would mean the world to me if you would accept this ring and become my wife. Monica, will you marry me?"

Between sobs, she could barely get the words out. She wiped the tears from her left cheek, then the right.

"Yes, Jamel! Yes! Yes! Yes! I will marry you!" she yelled. Pulling Jamel up from the pavilion floor, she wrapped her arms around his neck. They exchanged a long passionate kiss as their best friends and parents erupted into applause and words of love.

"Oh my God. I can't believe you did all of this for me!" she yelled. "Brenda! Nate! Where did you two come from?"

"Please call us Mom and Dad. We're about to be family," said Brenda. "Jamel flew us all in earlier today. There's no way that either of us would have missed this moment.

Monica hugged the four parents very tightly.

"Dad, are you okay?" she asked. Monica could feel moisture on his face.

"Yes, baby. I'm just overjoyed right now. My baby's getting married", said Toni.

"We're so happy for you, baby," said Tonya. "I knew this day would come. I just didn't know when. I've been praying about it for a long time now."

"Jamel is a good man. You two deserve all the happiness in the world and I'm so glad you allowed us to be a part of it," said Brenda.

"Mom, you know there was no way that I would let you miss it. I'm only doing this once, so you had to be here," said Jamel. "Everyone, please have a seat. Chef Jacques has prepared quite a meal for this occasion."

The violinist played through the entire dinner hour. The group sat around under the moonlit sky and enjoyed the evening by candlelight. The breeze from the ocean was intoxicating. This was by far the most incredible night so far. Monica looked at her left ring finger at the beautiful diamond ring Jamel had given her. She couldn't help but smile at the thought of becoming Mrs. Jamel Martin some time in her near future. She looked at Keisha who was staring adoringly at her best friend.

"Life is good," Keisha whispered.

"Yes, it is," Monica whispered back.

Monica moved to the other side of the table to take a seat next to Keisha.

"You know you have to be my Matron of Honor, right?"

"You know, I wouldn't have it any other way, right?"

The two women smiled. Monica knew that her life would forever be changed. Each day with Jamel had been better than the one before. He was truly a blessing from God and she would honor him until she took her last breath. She was already imaging what their wedding would be like. She could envision a couple of babies, and the happily ever after that most women only imagined. She was living the dream.

29 SOONER THAN LATER

Monica and Jamel walked down the moonlit beach with his hand in her left and her shoes in her right.

"Remember our walk down the beach in St. Thomas? It was the night I knew I was in love."

"Yes, I remember. You actually knew it that night?"

"Yes, I did. I had always seen something very special in you. I just needed you to see it too."

"I still can't believe we're getting married!" Monica turned to face him while taking steps backward through the sand. She stopped, forcing Jamel to stand in front of her.

"Babe, this has been the most amazing experience I've ever had."

"This trip? You haven't seen anything yet, future Mrs. Martin."

"Not just this trip. Every day since we began this relationship has been something out of a dream. I never imagined that life could be like this. That love could be like this. Every day, I just want to live in the moment because every moment with you has truly been magical."

They shared a long kiss under the stars before continuing down the beach until they ran into Darius and Keisha.

"You guys okay out here?" Darius asked.

"We couldn't be better. How are you guys doing?"

"The same. Man, that was some proposal. I'm so proud of you. So happy for both of you."

Keisha smiled at Monica before grabbing her arm.

"Have you guys thought about the date yet?"

"We've only been engaged for five minutes, but the truth is; yes, I have thought about it."

"What do you have in mind, love?" asked Jamel.

"I've always wanted to have a Spring wedding. What about some time next Spring? Next May, to be exact."

"If that's what you want, Babe. Then May it is."

"I'll call the church when we get back home to see what Saturday in May is available. Then we can start making the arrangements. Keisha, are you ready for this? I'm going to need you."

"Yes! I'm so excited! I cannot wait! Jamel, promise me that you're not taking my friend away from me." Keisha said.

"Girl, this will probably bring you two closer together; as if you could get any closer."

"We can take family vacations together. Our kids can play together. This is so exciting!"

"Okay, Keisha. Tell us how excited you really are!" Darius laughed. "Man, see what you've done?"

"I see. Anything for my queen. Whatever she wants."

"Where are the parents?"

"They're back at the house talking. Our Moms are probably having the same conversation we're having. Probably talking wedding talk if I know them like I think I do."

"Yeah, I can see that. Well, look at it like this. You won't have to do too much planning with your Mom, Monica's Mom, Monica and Keisha doing all of it. You'll just have to pick out a tuxedo and show up."

Jamel laughed, "No, I'm going to plan the honeymoon. Once she tells me where she wants to go, I'll get on it."

"I'm not sure what you can do to top this, though. You've definitely set the bar very high."

"Yeah, you're right. I'll think of something, though. You know I will."

"You've already proven that. I know you will, dude. If you need me to do anything, you know I'm here for you."

The foursome turned around to head back to the house. It was time for the dessert hour. Chef Jacques had prepared three of his specialties upon Jamel's request. He had also hired the Calypso band to return for a few hours, so they could get in some dancing while the night was still young.

"Man, I have definitely got to step up my game. I'm learning from the best. I've put my wife through so much that she deserves to be treated better than I treat her."

"Darius, you're doing a good job; but if you want some tips I'd be happy to share," Jamel laughed.

Darius looked at his friend. "Yes, I need to get better. She deserves more than this and I can afford to do more. I'm just not as romantic as you. I thought I was, but you've shown me a new side to romance that I didn't even know existed. I am your humble student."

"Man, you're crazy! But just watch and learn. Watch and learn, my brother."

The two men walked back up the beach a few steps behind the ladies.

"Look at them. They're in their own world now. We have two monsters on our hands."

"No, man. We have two queens. Don't forget it. Two queens. That's lesson number one."

Darius shook his head at Jamel. He was serious about his woman. He realized that he really could learn some lessons just by watching him. He was romantic but in a ghetto sort of way. Jamel was a class act. He was a lot more cultured than Darius. The good thing is Darius recognized it as something that was good and wasn't envious. He just wanted his wife to feel as special as Monica had been feeling. She deserved it too. He vowed to change, even if it meant getting help from Jamel to make it happen. Jamel's mind could conceive things that Darius had never thought of. If that's what it took, that's what it would be. Jamel could make him more cultured just like him. He made a mental note to spend more time with his friend. In fact, he intended on the four of them spending more time together. He would be his understudy. He was also going to be his best man and didn't want Jamel to be disappointed by anything he did or suggested for the wedding or any of the events leading up to it. Jamel was truly like a brother to him, even though Keisha was the one who had brought them together. She was the foundation for all the relationships and friendships that they shared.

30 A FEW MORE DAYS IN PARADISE

Keisha awoke to the sound of the rain hitting the deck floor. She rolled over and snuggled closer to Darius.

"Well, it's raining. I guess we'll be staying in this morning."

"I hear storms here don't last that long. It's pouring down right now, but I'll bet it stops within an hour or two."

"We'll see, but for now, I'm in no rush to get up. I smell breakfast, but I'm going to stay right here for about another hour if that's okay."

"Sure, babe. Are you feeling okay?"

"Yes, I'm good." Keisha lied.

Late last night, she started experiencing some pain in her legs but dismissed it as the after effect of the long walk they took on the beach. It's more difficult to walk on sand than it is to walk on a regular surface.

"If you weren't, would you tell me?"

"Yes, I would. My legs are a little sore, but that's it."

Darius grabbed one of her legs and began to give her a massage.

"What do you need me to do?"

"You're doing it."

He grabbed the lotion bottle from the nightstand and filled the palm of his hand with some of the tropical scented moisturizer.

Darius stroked both of Keisha's legs gently. "Does that feel good?"

"Yes, it does, babe. Thank you."

"Roll over."

Darius massaged her shoulders, and then her back.

"How about if I run you a nice bubble bath. It'll probably help your joints."

"Yes, that sounds good."

Darius jumped up from the bed and headed into the bathroom. He turned on the water in the tub before squeezing in the coconut and pineapple scented bubble bath. He removed Keisha's negligee before picking her up into his arms and placing her gently into the tub. He turned on the jets.

"How does that feel?"

"Amazing. Thanks, babe."

"Do you want me to get in with you?"

"There's enough room for an entire family in here. Yes, that would be good."

Darius thought about his conversation with Jamel last night on the beach.

"What do you think about going on a ski trip this winter? I mean, not to ski. We can take in some of the other activities like tubing, or snowmobile riding. Maybe we can invite Jamel and Monica. We can rent a big cabin and spend a few days out there."

"Wow, Darius. That sounds like fun! We've never done anything like that before."

"Well, my queen. It's about time we start."

"What about the girls?"

"No need to worry about them. I'll take care of everything."

Keisha smiled. "I would absolutely love that. Thanks, babe."

"You don't have to thank me. You deserve it. We can talk

about it with Jamel and Monica at breakfast."

"Sounds like a plan. Maybe you could invite a few of your single friends too. I'd love to invite Pam, Cynthia, and Shawn. We haven't all hung out in a while."

"Yes, that sounds good too. You rest here for a while. I'll lay out something for you to wear."

"Wow, thanks, babe."

"Anything particular you want?"

"No, you decide. Shorts and a t-shirt will work considering it's raining right now. We probably won't stray too far from the house."

Darius kissed her gently on the lips and then on her forehead before exiting the tub. He called and checked on the girls before getting their clothes ready for the day. Darius was determined to be a better man. He had done so much damage that he had to figure out a way to do better by the woman he would be spending the rest of his life with.

"No more drama," he thought. "You okay in there, baby cakes?"

"Yes, I'm fine. I think I'm ready to get out now, though. My fingers are shriveling."

"Okay, here I come," he laughed.

He scooped her up from the tub and laid her on a towel on the bed he'd placed there especially for her. At the foot of the bed rested a hot pink t-shirt with denim shorts, and hot pink bra and matching panties. He headed to the closet and returned with a pair of hot pink Jimmy Choo sandals.

"Where did these come from?"

"I picked them up from Tyson's Corner before the trip. I wanted to surprise you."

"They're beautiful. My favorite color. Thanks, babe."

Keisha slipped her feet into the sandals to try them on. "These are hot! You did good, babe."

Darius smiled. He really did want to do better, and while he recognized that material possessions weren't everything, he also knew that Keisha liked the finer things in life and he wanted to shower her with as many of those things as he could. She deserved it. All of it.

"I'll be right back. You get dressed. Oh, I checked on the girls. They're both doing okay. Mom and dad send their love."

"Oh, okay. I was going to call them after I got dressed. Thanks."

Darius exited the room and headed downstairs to the dining area. Monica and Jamel weren't there.

"Where's everyone?" He asked Chef Jacques.

"Jamel was here a moment ago. He said everyone would be down in fifteen minutes."

Darius had never noticed Chef Jacques accent before today. He hadn't really said many words, but he had a thick Caribbean accent.

"Have you ever thought about working in the U.S.?" Darius asked.

"I've been there a few times for events. I've never thought of relocating there, but I love to get there every chance I get."

"Well, I'm planning a ski trip for my family and friends and was wondering if you would be interested in traveling with us to be our chef for the week. It'll be cold. Something I'm sure you're probably not used to, but you wouldn't have to go out for anything. I would make sure you had everything you need for the week. Are you married? You could bring your wife if that's the case."

"I would definitely consider something like that. We can discuss the details later."

"Thanks, man. We would really love to have you and some of your delicious dishes. My man, Jamel has shown me a different side of life. I want to make sure that my wife experiences some more of it."

"That's right. Life is too short. You must show her all the love you can while you're here on this earth. Yes, my wife and I would love to be a part of the ski vacation. I'll pull out some of my finest dishes for you," he said in his island dialect.

"That sounds like a plan. I'd better check on my wife. We'll be down for breakfast in a few minutes. Thanks again,

Chef Jacques."

"Please, call me Jacques."

Darius smiled before exiting the dining area to return to his bride. She stood in front of the mirror putting on her jewelry. She was an angel and he was so thankful to have her.

"Is everything okay?"

"Yes, breakfast will be served in ten minutes. Are you ready?"

"I sure am, Mr. Kingston."

He grabbed Keisha's hand and escorted her out of the room and down the stairs. The others appeared shortly.

"Good morning, everyone," Keisha greeted her friends and the parents. "How's everyone doing?"

"Good morning, Keisha. We're great. We were checking out the pool."

"I forgot there was an indoor pool here. I'll have to check it out later. Darius, maybe we can take a swim later this evening. What do you think?"

"That sounds good, babe."

"Monica, how are you? Are you still in shock about everything that happened last night?"

"Girl, you know I am."

"Jamel, Keisha and I were talking this morning. We want to invite you guys on a ski vacation this winter. What do you think?"

"Wow, that's different. Yeah, why not? When are you thinking about going?"

"I was thinking sometime around the Martin Luther King holiday. That's a long weekend. We could tack a couple of days on to the front or back ends of the holiday."

"Monica, what do you think?" Jamel looked at his fiancé.

"Yes, I would love to do something like that. I don't know how to ski, though."

"Girl, neither do we! We're not going for the skiing. Darius was thinking about other ski activities and just some time to spend shut in a warm cabin in front of a nice fire while the winter weather does whatever it's going to do during that time. Maybe it'll even snow. Think about how romantic that would be."

"Yes, I see the vision," said Jamel. "Count us in. Just let me know what I need to do."

"You don't need to do anything. I'm planning this one. You just need to show up with your ski suit and your woman. I'll take care of the rest."

"Well alright then. It sounds like our next vacation is already in the works. Thanks, man."

"Jamel, after all of this; it's the least I can do."

"You guys bringing the kids?"

"No. No kids. This is a romantic getaway for us. Adults only. Just a time for us to relax and enjoy some time together. Besides, I was thinking about planning a trip to Disney World next year for the girls. Something they can enjoy. The ski trip is for us. Once you two start having babies, we'll plan more family-friendly trips that include all of the kids."

"That sounds like a good idea, Darius. I can't wait!"

"For the ski trip?"

"Well, yes; but I was thinking about babies."

Jamel smiled at Monica. He was ready too.

31 HOME

Darius turned the key in the door lock after parking the car in the garage. There was a coldness that filled the room that sent chills over his body. If he felt it, he was certain Keisha would too because she was always cold.

"I had a great time, but it sure feels good to be home."

"Yes, I feel the same way. There's nothing like sleeping in your own bed," Keisha said. "Let me put Keyana down and I'll unpack our things.

"Don't worry about it, babe. I still have to get the rest of the bags out of the trunk anyway. I'll be right back."

Darius began scanning the bag of mail they'd picked up from the post office on the way in. The light bill, gas bill, phone bill; a bunch of junk mail that he immediately through into the trashcan. Suddenly, an envelope caught his attention. It was addressed to them both. It was from Antonio. Darius opened the envelope.

Dear Keisha and Darius,

I hope you two had a great vacation. Daria is doing great. In fact, we both are. I wanted to know if the two of you had time to come down to Atlanta over the next couple of weeks, even if just for a weekend. I think it's time for the two of you to get to know her. I'm getting to a place where I can finally accept the inevitable. I just want her to be happy.

Anyway, just give me a call when you get a moment so that we can discuss the visit. I'm hoping that you bring Keyana with you so that the two of them can begin to get to know one another too. After all, they're sisters.

Thanks,

Antonio

Darius sat the letter on the family room coffee table. He thumbed through three photos that were enclosed. He knew Antonio was right. It was time for him to begin the process of getting to know his daughter. She also deserved to get to know him and his family.

"What's wrong?" Keisha sensed it as soon as she walked into the room.

"Nothing's wrong," he handed her the note from Antonio.

Keisha read the note intently before placing it on the table. She picked up the photos, staring at each one for several minutes.

"She's a cute little girl. She sort of favors Keyana," she admitted. "He's right. It's time to start this process."

"Are you sure you're okay with all of this?"

"Darius, I told you I was. Remember, nothing just happens so I believe she's here for a reason. God will reveal it all in due time. So, yes I am perfectly fine with it and I agree with Antonio. We need to get down there as soon as possible."

"Okay. I'll look at my schedule when I get back to work on Tuesday. Not this weekend, but maybe the next one. We could all fly down there. I'll call to make sure that it's a good time for him."

"Now can you get the bags out of the car before I rescind my offer to put everything away?"

"Oh, so you've got jokes I see."

He kissed Keisha's forehead before heading back into the garage.

"God knows how much I can take," she said to herself.

The remainder of the evening was quiet. Keyana played with several of the toys her grandparents had bought while she was staying with them.

"Kids are funny! You give them something new and it's as if nothing else existed. "I'm sure she hasn't even thought about any of the toys upstairs in her toybox."

"Well, Darius. That just means we have to stop buying her so much stuff. It's okay, though. Daria might find interest in some of it when she gets here. I'm sure some of it will be stuff she's never seen before, so it'll seem new to her, but I bet you Keyana will find interest in it again as soon as that happens."

"That's how kids are, right? They don't want it until they see someone else with it. It's definitely going to be interesting."

"I received a call from DJ. He wants to fly out here soon. I was thinking maybe we could take him to Atlanta with us. I haven't broken the news to him yet, but he needs to know. He needs to get to know both of his little sisters."

"That's a good idea. I miss him so much anyway. Yes, let's plan on taking him."

Keisha's mind wandered to the first day she ever saw the little boy who had become quite the young man. So polite and respectful. During the years he'd lived with Darius, she knew he'd probably seen some things that a child should never have to see. There were drunken binges, and probably a mirage of women in and out of the place before she came into his life.

"Did DJ ever meet Stephanie?"

"I had a feeling you would eventually ask me that. Yes, he met her once. She was a friend before the one-night encounter, remember? So, she had been around a few times. Do you really want to talk about this?"

"No, I was just wondering. I figured the answer would be yes. So, I guess explaining how Daria got here will not be as difficult as I thought."

"Probably not that difficult, but if it'll make you feel any better; DJ didn't like her at all. He was very respectful, but in one visit he told me that there was something up with her."

"Are you serious?"

"As a heart attack. He said he didn't like her and that there was something strange about her. Then he went on to say that I was supposed to be with you, and no one else. I should have listened."

"That's my boy," Keisha smiled. "One thing's for certain. DJ has always been in my corner."

"Keisha, that boy adores you. His mother says he's always talking about you. It's a good thing the two of you have a good relationship, too. Otherwise, she might get jealous."

"Yes, I suppose that is a good thing."

"Babe, why don't you get changed into something more comfortable. We can put Keyana to bed and spend some quiet time. Just the two of us."

"Yeah, that sounds good."

Keyana splashed around in the tub while Keisha washed her chubby little body.

"You look just like your daddy. What a cutie."

Keyana looked intently at her mother as if she knew exactly what she was saying.

"You're going to have a playmate very soon. A big sister. How does that sound? Can you say, Daria?"

"Da-ya! Da-ya!" she said.

"That's close enough for now. I actually like it," Keisha laughed.

Darius stood in the bathroom door admiring his wife and daughter.

"That's a good woman right there," he said while walking to their bedroom.

He ran water in the bathtub before squeezing in the bubble bath. He lit the six candles that lined the tub's shelving and three that were on a tray between the two sinks. He lit one on the dresser and one on the nightstand before removing his clothes.

"Babe, what are you doing? Trying to spend some time with my lovely wife, what do you think?"

"I think I like it," she stepped out of her jeans and sweater.

"Come on, I ran a bath."

Darius held her hand as she stepped into the hot water before getting in behind her.

"This is nice, isn't it? We don't use it enough."

Darius picked up the remote and hit the play button. *Thank You in Advance* by Boyz II Men began to play in the background.

"Wow, Darius. You're taking it way back!"

"Do you remember what I said to you when we first met?"

"How could I forget? You asked me what my first name was, but you called me Mrs. Kingston. I remember joking with you about this song," Keisha smiled.

"Yes, I knew you were going to be my wife someday. I didn't realize that we were going to go through all of the stuff we've been through, but love definitely endures, doesn't it?"

"Yes, babe. Love endures all things. True love never fails. It never dies. We've been through a lot, but you want to know something?"

"What's that?"

"I cannot imagine my life without you and if I have to go through these things with anyone, I'm so glad it's with you."

The couple ended the night making love quietly and slowly before exiting the tub. Keisha loved Darius more than she'd loved any man and she knew the love he had for her was beyond anything she could have ever pondered up in her wildest dream. Keisha exited the tub and towel dried her body before heading into the bedroom.

Wow, babe. What is this?"

On the bed laid the prettiest hot pink lace negligee from Victoria's Secret she'd ever seen.

"Something I picked up before we went on vacation. I intended on bringing it, but I knew you had already mapped out your vacation wardrobe. I'm glad I didn't now, because this seems like the perfect opportunity to present it to you."

Darius held the thong panties in his hand so that she could step in. Then he placed the negligee gently over her head.

"Look at you. My show stopper."

She looked in the mirror at her reflection. "It's beautiful."

"Just a small complement to your amazing figure and caramel colored skin."

He grabbed her from behind with the box in his hand. "I got you something else."

"Darius, what did you do?" She sat down on the bed and began removing the beautiful wrapping paper from the box. Darius removed the dainty Rolex and placed it on her wrist.

"I bought you this while we were in Turks and Caicos."

"Babe, you didn't have to do that. It's absolutely beautiful!"

"Not as beautiful as you. It's inscribed."

He removed it from her wrist so that she could see what was on the inside of the band.

Love endures all things. Even the tests of time. Love Darius

Keisha wrapped her arms around her husband's neck. "I love you so much, Darius Kingston. More than you could ever truly know."

They climbed into bed for a peaceful evening together, enjoying the intimacy that had only grown between them over the years before falling asleep. Keisha wished they could stay in that moment forever.

32 CYNTHIA

The group entered the ballroom at the Gaylord Hotel. Black evening gowns seemed to be the theme for the ladies, so Keisha stood out in her raspberry-colored gown that hugged her body in all the right places.

"Cynthia, I'm sure glad you decided to wear red tonight or else I'd be standing out like a sore thumb," she whispered.

"What in the heck did the invitation say to wear?" Cynthia said as she scanned the room.

"It just said black tie," Monica said as she handed her cell phone to Cynthia to view the electronic version of the invitation. "There weren't as many black dresses last year."

"Keisha, we'll be right back," Darius said as he and Jamel walked away to talk to another manager.

"I can't imagine there would be any single guys at this event, and if there are; they probably didn't come alone."

"Cynthia, you'd be surprised at how many of them fly solo at these events."

"I guess we'll find out soon."

The ladies headed toward the bar to grab drinks before claiming a table near the center of the room.

"See, what did I tell you," Keisha whispered to Cynthia while discreetly pointing at a handsome man headed in their "direction.

"Keisha, how are you? Where's that husband of yours?"

"Hi, Terrence. He's around here someplace. Let me introduce you to a good friend. You've met Monica before, right?"

"Yes, I remember meeting you a few times," Terrence kissed her hand.

"Okay, well this is Cynthia."

"Well, hello beautiful."

Terrence held onto her hand tightly while very obviously sizing her up.

"Where have you been hiding?"

"I haven't been hiding at all," Cynthia blushed.

"Can I get you something from the bar?"

"I could use a glass of cranberry juice," she said while slowly pushing the one she just got in Monica's direction.

Monica smiled, picked up the glass and began to drink from it.

"Well, would you like to accompany me?"

Terrence realized that he was still holding her hand, so he gently released it.

"I'd love to."

"Wow! We've been in the room for ten minutes and she's already found an eligible bachelor," Monica laughed. "He is single, right?"

"Yes, he divorced Erica at least a year ago. Remember her? As soon as he would leave town on business, she'd be seen all over town with that D.C. cop."

"Oh, yeah! That's right; I do remember that. It's a good thing he got rid of her. She was no good for him."

"There's Joel and Brian right over there too. The eligible men are definitely in the place."

The band began to play *Hello*, by Adele although Keisha preferred Joe's version only because she was one of his biggest fans.

"Come on, let's dance!"

Keisha and Monica headed toward the dance floor to be met by Darius and Jamel.

"Did you think I was going to let you dance by yourself?" Jamel asked.

"I wasn't going to dance alone. Keisha was right there," Monica teased as she turned her back to Jamel and danced closely behind him.

"I cannot wait to marry you," he whispered in her ear.

"Next May will be here before we know it," she said.

Jamel had been doing a good job of honoring Monica's wishes to not have any sexual contact until after they were married beyond their initial experiences, but the more time he spent with her the more difficult it became. The band began to play *I Want You*, by Marvin Gaye.

"You have got to be kidding me," Jamel laughed.

Monica laughed with him. "Babe, the time is really flying by. I'll be walking down the aisle before you know it. The lead singer is really doing her thing," she tried to change the subject.

Terrence and Cynthia were now on the dance floor. He stared into her eyes as they danced. He was enthralled with her.

"I'm surprised I haven't been introduced to you before," he whispered in her ear.

"I've been so busy with work, that I haven't been getting out much, so I'm not surprised."

"So, what do you do?"

"I'm a project manager on a government contract. I'm at the Pentagon."

"Oh, okay. I would love to get to know more about you, if you're not already with someone, that is."

"No, I'm actually not with anyone and yes, I would love that," Cynthia smiled.

The two walked off the dance floor together and took a seat at the table where he found them.

"Can we exchange information?"

"Yes, that would be great. Is your airdrop enabled?"

Terrence checked his phone to make sure that it was on. "I'm ready."

The two quickly exchanged contact information.

"I was going to make my rounds to talk to some of the

guys. You're welcome to join me. It looks like your girls are having a ball on the dance floor and I don't want to leave you sitting here all by yourself. Besides, as soon as I walk away I'm certain one of the guys will come over here to talk to you," Terrence admitted.

"Sure, I don't mind. I'll go with you," Cynthia said.

He seemed to be a nice guy. Someone she would be interested in spending more time with, but she wanted to talk to Darius before making her determination as to how much time she would spend with him; if any time at all. Especially after what she'd already been through. She made a mental note to talk to him about it on the ride home.

Cynthia spent most of the evening in Terrence's company. Enough time to learn that he was a divorcee with two little girls that he spent time with every other weekend and a month during the summers. Though a few other men had shown interest in her throughout the evening, she really liked Terrence.

"I sure hope he checks out," Cynthia whispered.

"What did you say?" Keisha asked.

"Oh nothing, we'll talk about it in the car."

Darius smiled. He already knew where this was going.

33 TERRENCE & CYNTHIA

Terrence arrived at Cynthia's house around 6:00 P.M. for their first date. She had agreed to go out with him after Darius gave the all clear. She found out that he was a really nice guy who was very attentive to his children. He loved being married but ended up with the wrong woman. One who didn't appreciate him. Erica didn't even respect him. According to Darius, he was not abusive, he wasn't a womanizer, and he was a hard-working manager who was steadily climbing the ladder within the FAA.

"You look amazing," he said as he handed her the bouquet of red roses he'd ordered earlier that day from the florist.

"Awe, thank you, Terrence. These are beautiful!" Cynthia tilted her nose toward the tip of the roses. The aroma was already beginning to occupy her space.

"So, I made us a reservation at McCormick & Schmick's down at the National Harbor. I asked Keisha if she thought you'd like it and she said you guys had been there before. So, I hope that's okay."

"Terrence, yes. I love that place. What time is our reservation?"

"It's at 7:00. I figured we could walk down on the pier if

we get there early enough."

"That sounds very nice. Let me just grab a jacket and I'll be ready."

Cynthia could feel his eyes on her as she walked away.

"What are you looking at?" she teased.

"Just the most beautiful woman I've ever laid eyes on."

"Why thank you," she blushed.

After helping her into her jacket, the two headed out the door. Terrence hit the button on the keyless entry remote to the jet-black Jaguar parked in the driveway.

"Oh, my goodness! I have the exact same car. Mine is gray, though."

"I guess we have some things in common, huh?"

"It sure looks like it." He helped her into the car before taking his place in the driver's seat. "Well, at least I know you would have no trouble driving it if you ever had to."

"You've got that right. I guess you'd be comfortable driving mine too."

"Are you kidding? I'm comfortable driving anything," he admitted. "If you had a motorcycle in that garage, I could drive that too."

"Do you have one?"

"No, not anymore."

Cynthia was glad to hear that he didn't. She would have been nervous about him being on the road with it, not to mention she was afraid to ride one.

"Okay, I have a confession."

"What is it?"

"I grilled Darius about you before deciding whether I would go out with you or not."

"Okay? I guess I passed the background check because here we are. I have a confession too. I asked Keisha and Darius about you too."

"Oh yeah? What did they have to say?"

"Well, Keisha threatened to snap my neck if I didn't treat you right. She said you were a good woman, but your last relationship was toxic and that's why you were single. She said she was trusting me with you and that I better not disappoint her."

"Wow, she said all that?"

Terrence digressed in his mind, back to what Darius had told him.

"Man, she's a good lady. She just made a bad choice with that last knucklehead she dated."

"What do you mean? What did he do?"

"What didn't he do? That's probably the better question."

"Okay?"

"He abused her. He cheated on her. He did all kinds of stuff."

"So, do you think she's ready to start dating again after all that?"

"Man, I think dating is probably the best thing for her. The ex is doing hard time for what he did to her. She's good. In fact, she hasn't dated anyone at all since then. You're the first."

"I feel honored. She's beautiful and intelligent. She has a nice figure and has a lot of things going for her. I think I really like her, man."

"Well, after what you went through with Erica; you also deserve to be happy too. How do you think she'll take the news that you're seeing someone? She won't care, and if she does she better keep her feelings to herself. She didn't care when she was out there running around with more than one other dude."

"Yeah, you're right."

Terrence put their conversation out of his mind. He wanted to focus on her.

"So, how was your day?"

"It was good. How about yours?"

"It was excellent. I have to admit that I've been anticipating this moment all day."

"The truth is, so have I. I've been thinking about our date since you asked me a couple of days ago. It's such a beautiful night, too."

"I hadn't realized how beautiful it was until you opened your front door."

Cynthia turned to look out the window.

"Are you blushing? Don't tell me you're shy."

"No, just very flattered by your compliments."

"I speak the truth."

"Well, I'm glad you do."

"So, tell me some more about yourself. Have you ever been married?"

"No, I've never been married before."

"Have you ever thought about it?"

"Of course, I have. You did say we were going to McCormick & Schmick's, right?"

"Yes, why? What's wrong?"

"Oh, I was just making sure we weren't headed to the Justice of the Peace," she smiled.

"Oh, I see you've got jokes."

"I'm just kidding."

"All jokes aside, I would consider getting remarried. I won't let the terrible things that happened in my last marriage hinder my decision to do it again. I would marry the right woman in a heartbeat. What about you?"

"Yes, I too would consider marriage despite the hurt and pain that my last relationship brought me. That's a conversation for another day, but yes. I would get married."

"That's good to know. I've never been one for casual dating. Good women are hard to come by. When you find a good one, you have to jump in with both feet. That's what I believe anyway. I wished I'd believed it when I got married the first time. She was all wrong for me."

"Why did you say that?"

"We had nothing in common. She liked hanging out in the club and I liked spending quiet time together. I enjoyed working to support my family, but she loved spending everything I made. She didn't believe in saving anything for our future. Not even for the girls. She also didn't know how to stay faithful to the marriage."

"Keisha sort of mentioned that."

"I figured she would."

"Well, if it makes you feel any better; my last relationship was sort of like that. He didn't bring much too the table but took a lot.

"The truth is, Darius mentioned some it."

"Exactly how much did he tell you?"

"I don't know. You tell me."

"Did he tell you he cheated? That he beat and tortured me when I confronted him about giving me a sexually transmitted disease?"

"Wait, what? No, he didn't tell me all that."

"I'm only telling you because I really like you. You deserve to know."

"What exactly did he give you? Was it something you could get rid of or something you'll have to live with for the rest of your life?"

"No, it was a curable disease. I'm fine, now. One that just required a round of antibiotics and it was over, but I was embarrassed about even having to go through that up until just recently. I was beating myself up for falling for someone like him, but most importantly; for not protecting myself . . . my temple from him.

"Don't beat yourself up about it. Just think, it could have been much worse. I believe the things we go through in life are lessons that we must go through to make us stronger. Our struggles and challenges build strength and character. Think about what you learned from the experience and let it go. That's my take on every challenge that comes my way."

"So, you're not ready to run for the hills because of what I've shared with you?"

"Absolutely not. What kind of man would I be if I ran just because you went through some drama with the last man in your life? I really like you too, and I think you're worth getting to know better. We can take this as slow as you'd like. I just want to spend some time with you so that you can see that I'm genuine in what I say to you. Deal?"

"Deal."

Terrence kissed her hand, "now let's have a wonderful evening together."

Cynthia watched him circle the front of the car to get to the passenger's side. She smiled. He was a true gentleman and she really did want to get to know him better.

"We have a reservation for two. The last name is Burton."

"Good evening, Mr. Burton. Your table is ready. Please follow me."

Terrence again admired her as she followed the hostess to the table. She was a delicate, fragile flower that he wanted to not only spend more time with but love. Some people believe in love at first sight. He was one of them.

34 DARIA

Keisha and Darius exited the airport headed for the rental car. Keyana was fast asleep in his arms.

"That was nice of Antonio to let us stay at his place. Are you sure you're okay with that?"

"Yes, babe. It just makes sense. If we stay there, we can spend more time with Daria before heading back to Maryland. I'm just sorry that DJ couldn't make it."

"Yeah, me too. I miss him so much. I don't know, the more I think about it, it's probably best for us to do this without him. He can fly out to Maryland when Daria and Antonio come to town," Darius admitted. "If you change your mind any time during the visit about staying at Antonio's, just let me know and I'll get us a room at the Westin or someplace else. Just say the word."

"Stop worrying. He said he has a big place with plenty of room for all of us. I have absolutely no problem staying there."

Darius entered the address into the GPS, buckled his seatbelt and headed toward Cobb County.

"You nervous?" Keisha looked at Darius.

"I have to admit, I am a little."

Darius made a right turn into the development. Following the GPS commands, he then made a left.

"Wow! These houses are huge! He wasn't joking about having enough space for us."

"You're right about that. Look at the length of this driveway. The front yard alone looks like four or five acres of land."

"I'll get Keyana while you get the suitcases."

"Okay." Darius stood behind the car and admired the scenery. Antonio was definitely doing good for himself.

The maid answered the door on the second ring.

"Good afternoon, we're here to see Antonio Shaw?"

"Yes, he's been expecting you. Please come in," Helena said before escorting them to the family room.

Keisha admired the staircases on either side of the grand foyer. It was beautiful. She sat Keyana down on the floor and began looking at the photos lining the fireplace mantle. There were pictures of Daria all over the place. Then some of the two of them. There was even a family portrait of him, her, and Stephanie. Keisha removed it from the mantle and stared at it before putting it back in its place.

"You sure knew how to stir things up, didn't you?" she mumbled.

"Hey, you," Antonio said as he headed down the stairs with Daria in his arms. He put her on the floor next to Keyana.

"Antonio, man; this place is something else! You didn't tell us you were living the lifestyle of the rich and famous!" Darius laughed.

"It's home for us, man. You can get a lot more house for your money down here in the ATL. You know that."

"Well come on. I'll give you guys the grand tour. Helena, will you get Samantha to watch the girls for me?"

"Who's Samantha?" Keisha inquired.

"She's the nanny. She's been with us since Stephanie died. She lives here too, but when I'm home I take care of Daria myself. Helena lives here as well, so if you need anything she's here for you up until 7:00 P.M."

"Antonio, we don't want to be any trouble."

"You're no trouble, Miss," said Helena. "No trouble at all.

That's what I'm here for."

"After the tour, I have prepared some light hors d'oeuvres to hold you until dinner. So, please come to the dining room when you're ready."

"Helena, how about we end the tour there?" Antonio suggested.

"Sounds good. See you in a bit." She got down on the floor to entertain the girls while she waited for Samantha to appear.

"Keisha and Darius, here's your room. I brought Daria's crib from my parent's house so that Keyana would have a place to sleep. You have your own bathroom and sitting area. The closet is also empty if you want to hang up your clothes. The drawers in the dresser and chest are empty too. Please make yourselves at home. I'm really glad you came down."

"Antonio, we really appreciate your hospitality. This is definitely much better than staying over at the Westin."

"This is better than some resorts. Man, this place is something!" Darius said.

"Thanks, man. Business has been great. It affords me the opportunity to live like this. Daria doesn't want for anything. Neither of us do."

"I can see that," Darius scanned the room. Then headed toward the window. There's a pool out here too?"

"Yes, there's a tennis court further in the back also."

"I might have to challenge you to a game before we leave."

"Sounds good. I have to warn you, I play at least four times a week. You sure you're ready for it?" Antonio boasted.

"Yes, I'm ready. Keisha knows a little something too!"

"Don't be trying to put me in it. You're the one talking all the junk. You play!"

"All jokes aside. Let me show you to Daria's room. There are twin beds in there, so if you're comfortable with Keyana sleeping in there with her it's fine too. I have safety rails in her closet."

"Oh, my goodness! This is so adorable, Antonio."

There were little princesses all over the wall. Brown-faced princesses all wearing tiaras and cute little gowns that glistened when the light hit them. The ceiling had clouds painted on it and there were more princesses dangling from the ceiling like little angels coming down from heaven. There were pink curtains lining the three windows with matching comforters on both beds and in the crib. Keisha walked into the bathroom. There were more princesses everywhere.

"Antonio, this is beautiful. Who did this?"

"I designed the room, but Stephanie decorated it. Despite all the crazy things she did, she really did love Daria."

Keisha's eyes filled with tears. Looking around the room, it was evident that it was filled with a mother's love.

"The person I knew was nothing like the one you guys knew. She was loving and kind as long as she was taking her medication, but when she didn't," he hesitated. "When she didn't, you never knew what you might get. I've never felt the wrath of the Stephanie you knew, but I did have to pick her up from Lennox Mall one day when she didn't take her meds. She was out of control. Most days, I made sure she took the pills. Every now and then, she would hide them under her tongue and dispose of them because she didn't like the way they made her feel. That day, she was out of control. Way out of control."

"What was she taking medication for?"

"Stephanie was Schizophrenic and Bipolar. Didn't you know?" Antonio looked at Darius.

"No, I had no idea. I'd never seen the person who showed up in Maryland either. I knew there was something going on with her, but I didn't know it was that. Bipolar, maybe; but not Schizophrenic too. What about Daria? Is she okay?"

"Yes, she's fine. You have nothing to worry about with her."

"I guess I really didn't know her at all," Darius lowered his head in shame.

"It's okay, man. She hadn't been diagnosed when you knew her. She found out a couple months after we started dating. No one knew what she was really capable of until she pulled off that attack on Keisha."

"Well, I'm really sorry how it all turned out," Keisha admitted, "but had Monica not shot her, I might not be standing here today."

"There's no doubt about that. I understand why what happened had to happen. She was out of control. Unstoppable. I just wish I could have done more to help her. I really did love her, with her crazy self."

Keisha looked at Antonio with half a smile, "so how are you getting along without her?"

"I'm getting along just fine. I must admit that sometimes I miss her. Sometimes, I look at Daria and realize that she'll never know the woman I had come to know. I feel bad because little girls need their moms. That's one of the reasons why I felt this visit was necessary. Keisha, she's going to need you. I know you've been put in an awkward position, but she's going to need a mother. There are just some things I can't teach her. Only a mother can teach her how to be a young lady. How to love like only a mother can, and while it is going to break me when I have to let her go, I want what's best for her."

"It looks like you've been providing a very good life for her right here."

"Yes, I have; but I can't buy her a mom."

"I get that. You're right. She does need a mom. I couldn't imagine leaving Keyana behind to make it in this life without me."

Keisha stood closer to Darius and placed her head against his arm. "You okay, babe?"

"Yes, I'm fine. I'm just taking this all in. That's all."

"We better get back downstairs. Helena will get upset if we don't eat the food she prepared. I guess one of her gifts is cooking for others. That's how she shows her love, so let's get going."

Darius and Antonio scooped up the girls who were playing together very peacefully, and the group headed into the kitchen to wash their hands before moving into the dining room.

35 DARIA & DADDY

Keyana's expression confirmed that she wasn't sure what to make of Daria sitting on her daddy's knee. She watched cautiously as she made her rounds from one toy to another.

"I'm surprised she hasn't come over there," Keisha admitted.

"Yeah, I'm surprised too."

Daria touched Darius's bottom lip before putting her fingers into his mouth.

"She seems to be quite comfortable with you, man. She's usually not that welcoming.

Although Darius was still a little uncomfortable with the inevitable, he knew he'd better get used to it fast. It was just a matter of time before this would be the new normal. The truth was, that he was more concerned with Keisha waking up one day and realizing that this wasn't what she signed up for. He feared her taking Keyana and walking away.

"Lunch is ready, everyone," Helena announced before exiting the room.

Darius put Daria down, took her hand in his right and Keyana's hand in his left and led them both into the kitchen. Keisha and Antonio followed closely behind.

"You okay?" Antonio asked in a whisper.

"Yes, I'll be fine."

"I know this is a lot, right?"

"It sure is, but I also truly believe that God will never give you more than you can handle. Thinking back, I don't believe this is the most difficult I've seen. I'm good."

Keisha thought back to the many times she'd been hospitalized. Besides the events that took place at the house with Stephanie, she hadn't been in there in quite a while. For that, she was very thankful.

"Dear Lord, we thank you for this meal that Helena has prepared for us. Thank you for this opportunity for us all to get to know one another better and I pray that you will guide us through making the right decision for Daria. These things I ask in your Holy name, Amen."

"Amen," said Keisha.

"Amen," Darius smiled.

Helena had prepared a delicious chicken salad with fresh fruit, pickle slices, deviled eggs, and potato salad.

"Helena, everything is so good!" Darius said to break the silence.

"Thank you, sir. Thanks for telling me that Keisha is allergic to celery. I would have normally added some, but this time I didn't. I actually think it tastes better this way."

"Yum!" Keyana said before stuffing a piece of her chicken salad sandwich into her mouth.

"Yum!" said Daria.

Everyone laughed.

"I think we may have a case of monkey see, monkey do on our hands. I wonder if this is how it's going to be from here on out?"

"I'm sure we're probably in store for a lot of it," said Darius.

"I was thinking in a couple of hours, we could head over to Six Flags. Do you think the girls would like that?"

"They're still young. I wonder if they'll even care?" Keisha asked.

"Well, they have a section over there for younger kids. I think they would enjoy it. Besides, I'm interested in seeing them interacting in a fun environment," Antonio admitted.

"Yeah, I hadn't really thought about that. We really need to get them interacting in different environments so that they can get used to being with each other."

"Tomorrow, I've planned a backyard barbeque. I ordered a moon bounce for the kids, a clown, and a face painter. I invited some of my business associates and their families who also have small children. I think it will be a lot of fun."

"Sounds like a plan," said Darius. "You've thought of everything, I see."

"I was just trying to figure out some things that we could do while you guys were here. I figured next month, we'll take a trip up to Maryland. I've never done the DC tour. You think you guys will have time to hang out with us?"

"Of course. Yes, that sounds great. There's a place called My Gym in Waldorf that I would like to take them to. I think they would enjoy it," Keisha said. "It's not far from the hotel you stayed in the last time you came up."

"I believe I saw it when Daria and I went out to grab something to eat. It's in a shopping center near the mall."

"Yes, that's the place. Keyana and I go there sometimes. We were introduced to it when one of her little friends from her regular play date had a birthday party over there."

"Okay, a DC tour and a gym date. I'm looking forward to it," Antonio said.

"Sounds like you're looking forward to it more than the kids," Darius laughed.

"Anything for the babies."

"Antonio, I'm going to get Keyana changed for the trip out to Six Flags. Do you want me to get Daria ready too?"

"No, Samantha can . . . you know what? Yes, you can do that if you'd like."

Keisha took the girls upstairs to get them changed into clothing that would be more comfortable for the park.

"I'm so glad we brought your stroller."

Keyana looked at her mother and laughed. After she was changed into her hot pink jeggings and matching sweatshirt,

Keisha found a similar outfit in Daria's closet. Everything was so well organized. Her little outfits were color-coded and hanging on little pink hangers.

"I never would have imagined that Stephanie was this creative," Keisha whispered out loud. "She did a great job on all of this."

Keisha grabbed the girl's jackets before heading back downstairs.

"Awe! Don't they look adorable," said Darius.

"I guess these are daddy's girls, huh?"

"I guess they are," Keisha said.

"Antonio, Daria's lucky to have two dads, isn't she?" Darius asked.

Antonio smiled. In his heart, she would always be his daughter, but he had accepted the fact that she wasn't his biological daughter and he was going to have to let go a little.

"Man, you're going to get so tired of me showing up in Maryland to see how she's doing. I hope you don't mind."

"Not at all. We can share the responsibility of raising her. She's blessed to have us all."

"Yes, she is. The car should be here shortly. I was going to drive, but I'm going to have my driver take us over there and pick us up."

"A driver? Okay."

Five minutes later, the black Denali made its way up the driveway and parked in front of the door. The driver jumped out and opened the passenger front and rear doors.

"Curtis, I'd like you to meet Keisha and Darius. This little lady here is Keyana."

"Hi, it's nice to meet you. Welcome to Atlanta."

"Thanks, Curtis," Keisha said as he extended his hand to help her get into the vehicle.

The group arrived at the park in 50 minutes. Keyana's face lit up. She looked from Keisha to Darius and then at Daria. She began to wiggle in her car seat. She wanted out. Daria looked at her and began to laugh. Then she began to wiggle in her seat too.

"Well, Antonio. It looks like you were right," Darius admitted. "They're anxious to get out of this car."

"Curtis, we'll only be in the park for a couple of hours, but I'll give you a call about 45 minutes or so before we're ready to head out of here."

"Sounds good, Antonio. I'll see you guys a little later."

They headed into the park where they had a great afternoon watching the girls ride the kiddie rides while getting to know each other better.

36 STRANGER BY THE MINUTE

Keisha rolled over as she heard the rev of a truck engine nearby. She climbed out of bed and headed to the window.

"Darius, it looks like Antonio's getting things set up for the party today."

"I guess we'd better get up. I'm going to check on Keyana and Daria."

Keisha stepped out of her nightgown, then turned on the shower. She stuck her fingers into the water stream before stepping in.

"Babe, I'm going outside to see if Antonio needs some help. The girls are still asleep!" He yelled.

"Okay, babe. Sounds good. I'll get them ready after I get ready."

Keisha heard her cell phone ringing as she turned off the shower. Wrapping a towel around her body, she grabbed it from the vanity.

"Hey, girl," Monica said. "How's it going down there?"

"Hey. It's going a lot better than I expected. Antonio has a beautiful home. He's got a nanny, maid, and a driver. He's having a huge barbeque today so that the girls can spend more time getting to know each other. He said he invited some people from his company who also have kids. It should be a lot of fun."

"Well, I'm certainly glad that everything is going well. How are the girls getting along?"

"Oh, they were so cute last night. We went to Six Flags yesterday and they were riding the rides together. Then last night, they started crying when it was time to go to bed. They didn't want to separate, so they slept in the same room."

"Awe! That's adorable. How's Antonio taking all of this?"

"He seems to be okay. I believe we'll be seeing a lot more of him. He's been a great father to her since Stephanie . . . well, you know."

"That's to be expected, right? Monica ignored the reference to Stephanie."

"Yes, I'd be concerned if he just disappeared on her. He's going to miss her, though. I can already see that."

"When are you guys heading back?"

"We're flying out on Monday."

"Oh, okay. I just wanted to check on you. I'll call you Monday evening. Jamel sends his love."

"Tell him hello and I love you guys."

Keisha looked at her image in the mirror. She was starting to look a little older lately. Most certainly because of some of the things they were going through, but she was still beautiful. It wasn't anything that a little bit of hair color and a spa day couldn't fix.

Keisha heard the door knob turn, but the door never opened.

"Who's there?"

"Mama!" Yelled a little voice from the other side.

"Keyana? How did you get in here? Daria, how did you get out of your crib?"

The girls both climbed onto the bed.

"I'm going to have to talk to Antonio about this. I'll bet he doesn't know you've figured out how to get out," she laughed.

Keisha put on her maxi dress, swooped her hair into a high ponytail and added a little bit of makeup before taking the girls back to Daria's room to get washed up and dressed. She found Samantha in Daria's closet picking out her outfit for the day.

"Good morning, Miss. I mean, Keisha. I hope you slept well. I was wondering where the girls were."

"Did you know that Daria could climb out of her crib?"

"Get out of here. No way!"

"Yes, the two of them just showed up in the other room a little while ago."

"No, I had no idea she could do that. We'll have to make sure Antonio knows. This house is so big that she could get lost if she gets out and he's not aware of it. He's got so much security around the windows and doors, that I wouldn't be concerned with her getting outside of the house; but there's a lot she could get into just wandering around this place."

"Okay. I'll be sure to mention it when I get outside. So, is this what Daria will be wearing today? It's cute. Keyana has an outfit almost like that. Hers is orange and yellow. Maybe I'll let her wear it today."

"Keisha, if you don't mind; may I ask you something?"

"Sure, Samantha. What's going on?"

"Well, Antonio mentioned that Daria would be going to live with you and Darius back in Maryland some time soon. I was wondering when you would be taking her? If I'm getting too personal, please let me know. It's just that I've been caring for her for a while now and I've gotten very attached to them. I mean her."

"Well, Samantha. We're not quite sure when she'll be moving, but yes; the plan is for her to move to our home in Maryland. Darius needs to get to know his daughter. While this situation is unique and a little unsettling for everyone involved. She's going to have to be uprooted from the only home and father she's known to live with someone who is really a stranger to her. It's unfortunate, but I believe it's the only way."

"I understand," Samantha lowered her head. It was obvious that she really cared about Daria.

"Samantha, do you mind if I ask you a question?"

"Sure."

"Did you ever meet Stephanie?"

"Of course. I knew her very well. She was my cousin."

"What?" Keisha's heart sank. "Are you serious?"

"Wait. Please let me finish. Stephanie was my first cousin, but we weren't that close. I actually knew Antonio from years ago. I used to be his secretary when he first opened his business. I left for another position, but when things didn't work out over there, and Stephanie died; he called to ask if I minded helping him out with Daria."

"I see. Wow, this story gets more interesting by the minute."

"Yes, I can see how you would feel that way. Antonio didn't feel comfortable leaving her with just anyone and he knew he could trust me. So, he hired me to be her nanny."

"So, what must the family be thinking about all of this?"

"The truth is, Stephanie was really like the black sheep of our family. She would do some of the craziest things. We didn't know she was ill. Everyone understands how she got herself in the position she ended up in. No one wanted to see her die, but she walked into that situation on her own."

"I wonder why Antonio didn't tell us that you were her cousin?"

"He was probably protecting me, and maybe even you too. Antonio mentioned that you were sort of caught in the middle of all of this. He didn't want to hurt or alarm you in any way. My biggest concern is Daria. I would never do anything to hurt anyone. Besides, as I said before; Stephanie had her issues and she brought it all on herself. I just pray she is at peace. That's all we can hope for anyway."

"You know, I didn't see it before, but the two of you do look alike."

"Our mothers are identical twins."

Keisha stared at Samantha in amazement.

"If I may say something else?"

"Sure, Samantha. You can say whatever you want."

"I really do care about Antonio a lot. Before Stephanie came along, back when I was working for him I used to imagine myself going on a date with him. I have always thought he was quite handsome. A good catch, but he doesn't even know I exist. It's probably because he used to be involved with Stephanie. I don't know. Maybe I'm not ambitious enough?"

"I don't know, Samantha. It may not be either of those things. Maybe he's just been so focused on raising Daria that he hasn't had time to notice? Have you ever thought about sharing your feelings with him?"

"Yes, I thought about it. Then he revealed what was going on with Daria. That she wasn't his daughter. He was so devastated. I just wanted to comfort him, so I put my feelings aside to make sure that he was okay."

"I can see you really have feelings for him. Probably more so than you've admitted to anyone before."

"Yes. I'm just waiting to see how it all plays out. I do wish Daria didn't have to leave, though."

"I'll tell you what. You're welcome to come to Maryland anytime with Antonio. I'll make sure he knows that."

"Keisha, thank you. You have such a warm spirit. That's why I felt comfortable talking to you about all of this. You didn't deserve to be caught in the middle. I'm so sorry for what Stephanie tried to do to you."

"It's okay, Samantha. I made it through. By the grace of God, I made it through."

"We'd better get the girls ready. The party will be starting in a little while."

"Yes! I'll be right back. I better check on Darius."

"Babe! You might want to start getting ready!" Keisha yelled as she headed toward Darius and Antonio.

"Yeah, man. It's probably time for both of us to get ready. The guys can handle the rest," said Antonio.

Keisha looked at Antonio. Suddenly, she felt a sense of sadness for him and the situation. He had no idea that there was a beautiful young woman in the house who was in love with him. She was in love with Daria too. Keisha concluded that Samantha wanted them to be a family. The fact that she's Stephanie's cousin could be a problem, though. The paternity results had thrown a monkey wrench right into the middle of her plan. Even if Antonio would have considered dating her, Daria was now leaving, which could potentially leave her out of a job. The whole situation was getting stranger by the minute.

37 MEET THE KINGSTON'S

The guests began arriving almost immediately after Darius finished getting dressed.

"Darius, you seem a little nervous. You okay, babe?"

"Yes, I'm fine. I had a good talk with Antonio while we were helping out in the back."

"What's going on? Is everything okay?"

"First, he has a fondness for Samantha."

"What? Now that you mentioned it. She's in love with him. We had a long talk too while we were getting the girls ready. She told me something that you're not going to believe."

"Yes, I would believe it. He told me about Samantha and Stephanie. I had no idea. Although, she does sort of resemble her."

"Yes, she does. So, what do you think? Do you think they'll end up hooking up?"

"Keisha, I don't know. I did tell him that he needs to follow his heart, though. Stephanie's gone. He can't bring her back. It is what it is."

"Yeah, that's for sure. She loves that little girl a lot."

"That's another thing we talked about. He asked me if I would consider leaving her here. He wanted to know if we would allow her to live here with him. He would raise her as a stepparent and then she would come to Maryland to visit with us from time to time."

"Darius, how do you feel about that?"

"I'm not sure how I feel about it. She is my daughter, but she doesn't even know me. She calls him Daddy and everything. This situation could be very confusing to her. I guess it could get very confusing to Keyana too as they both get a little older, but I don't know what to think or what to do at this point. I mean, how do you feel about all this?"

"Darius, it's not my decision to make. If you decide that she needs to come to Maryland to live, I'll support your decision 100 percent. If you decide that it's best for her to stay here in Atlanta, I'll support that too. At the end of the day, it's really all about what's best for Daria."

"I don't know. She has a good life here. Antonio has the means to provide her with anything she could want or need. If she comes to Maryland, you're going to have to end up taking care of them both while I work. It's a huge responsibility. I don't want to put too much on you."

"Darius, as I said. I'm prepared to do whatever you need me to do. If you decide to let her stay in Atlanta, we're going to have to come down here more often. You do realize that, don't you?"

"Yes, but Antonio will have to travel to Maryland more often too. It's all about give and take. We'll have to share the responsibility. I don't know. I'm going to think about all of it some more. I don't want to make a snap judgment decision on how this should go without thinking about it in the long term. Anyway, we could try it out for a while and maybe one day, she'll want to come anyway. I just don't want her to resent me. I don't want her thinking that I didn't want her. You know what I mean?"

"Yes, I do. I agree you should think about it some more. We'd better get outside. Antonio did all of this for us. We don't want to keep his guests waiting."

Darius and Keisha headed into the backyard with Keyana walking between them. She had gotten quite independent since realizing that she could get around faster if she walked. She still needed a little stability, so they each held one of her hands.

"Everyone, may I have your attention?" Antonio stood in the middle of the crowd. "I want you to meet a very special family. They came down from Maryland to hang out with us for the weekend. I'd like you to meet the Kingston's. This is Darius, Keisha, and their beautiful daughter, Keyana."

"Hi Darius, it's nice to meet you," said an older gentleman who had a woman who looked to be at least ten years his junior on his arm. "I'm Antonio's father, Will. This is my wife, Marissa."

"Oh, it's a pleasure to meet you both."

"Antonio has had a lot of nice things to say about both of you. He's a good guy, and I'm hoping you all can work this all out for Daria. She's such a precious gift, isn't she?"

"Yes, sir. She is. We're working through it. Right, Keisha?"

"Yes, Mr. Will. We're working through it as best as we can."

"Please, call me Will. He said, reaching for Keisha's hand.

"You're an angel. You've been dealt a unique set of circumstances, yet you're still hanging in there."

"Yes, Will. I suppose it is very unique, but Darius is my husband and I love him dearly. Besides, love endures all things. Isn't that what it says in the Bible? If we can make it through this, we can make it through anything. Lord knows we've been through some things. I'm sure you're aware of the circumstances that got us here, right? It's not ideal, but it's what we've all been dealing with."

"Yes, you're right. You've all been dealing with it, and quite well from what I can tell. Well, it was truly a pleasure meeting you. I'd better give someone else a chance to talk."

"Wow. He's an interesting fella," Keisha whispered.

"He sure is. Thanks for handling him the way you did. You shut him down."

"You'll have to excuse my father. He's a little high strung," Antonio admitted. He handed Daria to Samantha who was standing so close to him that their bodies were touching. "Let me introduce you to Chris and his wife, Chantel."

The couple was already making their way toward the group.

"Chris, it's good to see you. Chantel?" Antonio gave her a kiss on her cheek.

"Hi, it's a pleasure to meet you. You have a beautiful family."

"Thanks."

"Chris is one of the wealthiest minority business owners in the entire city of Atlanta. He owns a large portion of the commercial real estate in the downtown area. He recently purchased a condo community right down the street from Lennox Mall."

"It's nice to meet you, Chantel," Keisha extended her hand.

"It's a pleasure to meet you too."

"Chantel is a high-powered business attorney in the area."

"That's how the two of us met almost twenty years ago," Chris bragged. "I knew when I first laid eyes on her that she would be my wife. We just celebrated our fifteenth wedding anniversary last June."

"That's great! I'm looking forward to hitting some of the milestone anniversaries myself. Darius and I haven't been married that long."

"You'll get there. Just put God first in everything you do and everything else will fall right into place," Chantel offered.

"Thanks. That's some of the best advice I've heard in a while."

"Keisha, sorry to interrupt. Daria wants to ride the pony. Do you want to bring Keyana?" Samantha asked.

"Sure. If you would excuse me," giving Chantel a smile before she headed toward the pony with Samantha and the girls.

"I'll head in that direction with you. Chris Jr. is in the moon bounce. I'd better check on him. He'll stay in there forever if I let him."

"Oh, how old is your son?" Keisha asked.

"He just turned five. We have a seven-year-old daughter too. She's over there with the clown getting her face painted."

"Oh, how cute!" Keisha said as she focused her eyes on little Cheree who was getting a butterfly painted on her cheek.

"Keisha, just hang in there. Things will get better as time goes on. Antonio told us about what's going on. If you need anything, just someone to listen; I'm here."

"Why, thank you, Chantel. I really appreciate that."

"We faced some challenges early on in our marriage. The ratio of men to women down here in Atlanta is outrageous. We separated after our third year of marriage for a short time and Chris dated someone else. It took us a couple of years to finally get rid of her after he ended it to come back home."

"What did you guys end up doing?"

"Introduced her to Antonio's father. You just met Marissa a little while ago."

"Wait, what?"

"Yes, Marissa was Chris's mistress while we were on the outs. Now, she's married to Antonio's father."

"That seems a little awkward. How do you deal with it?"

"She's no competition to me. I don't compete with anyone. I don't have to. Besides, I'm the one he came back to. We don't have any problems out of her now that she's married to Will. In fact, he's the best thing for her. He's loaded and she's just a gold digger anyway. His money is a lot longer than ours," she laughed. "He knows how to keep her occupied."

"You've got a lot of confidence," Keisha admitted.

"You should too. Darius loves you. Antonio has talked about you two a lot. The fact that you're strong enough to be dealing with all of this says a lot about your strength and character. I admire that."

"Thank you, Chantel. I really needed to hear that."

"No problem, Keisha. The girls are both so adorable. So, what's going to happen next?"

"We're still trying to figure it all out. Antonio is so good to her. He loves her and it's going to be a difficult decision to make, but Darius will do what he feels right. I believe he will."

"You guys just take it to God. He'll give you the answers you need. Just listen."

"Here, take this," Chantel handed Keisha her business card. "Use it any time you need to. My business information is on the front, but my personal contact info is on the back. I'm here for you. Remember that. Besides, we come to the DC area at least a couple of times a year. Maybe we can get together sometime for dinner or just a friendly visit."

"That sounds wonderful. Yes, I would love that," Keisha hugged Chantel.

The two ladies watched Samantha holding both girls on the pony.

"They're so cute together. Regardless of what decision you guys make about this, they'll always be bonded as sisters."

"Yes, they will."

"Samantha's been a Godsend for Antonio. She's so good with Daria. She treats her like she's her own daughter. It's amazing how close they are."

"Yes, I see that. They are good together. Antonio's very blessed to have her."

"That cousin of hers was something else. I don't like to speak ill of the deceased, but she didn't mean Antonio any good."

"So, you knew her?"

"Knew her? Of course, I did. Chris and Antonio have been doing business together for a long time, but they've been friends even longer. We've all spent quite a bit of time together over the past couple of years. Stephanie was abusive to him. I remember once, we were having dinner here at the house. The next thing I knew, she had bashed him in the head with a cast iron skillet. He didn't tell you about it? It wasn't that long ago."

"No, he didn't mention it. Did he tell you guys about the time she showed up in Maryland? The first time?"

"Yes, he did."

"Well, I remember them arresting her because she was driving while under the influence of alcohol. They got her for stalking, and I remember something about an outstanding assault warrant."

"Yes, that would be the incident. After she hit him, she ran out of the house. Antonio was bleeding so badly that we had to rush him to the hospital. Once the ER doctor examined him, they contacted the police who charged her with assault after Antonio admitted what happened. He didn't want to press charges, but the State of Georgia did, and the warrant was issued."

"Wow! That's crazy!"

"It wasn't the first time. She'd assaulted him before, but never to the extent of the last one. There was so much blood, we were afraid he wouldn't make it. Not only that, but she cheated on him often. Don't get me wrong. Stephanie could be as sweet as pie, but if she didn't take her medication; you didn't know or like the person she could be."

"I'm surprised Antonio put up with all that. He doesn't seem like the type. I mean, look around. He can have any woman he wants."

"Yes, but he was in love with Stephanie. I overheard you tell Will a little while ago that love endures all things. You're right, it does. Antonio loved her and so he made the best of the situation. He was trying to help her, but I'm not sure I believe she wanted to be helped."

"Chantel, you've definitely shed some light on this entire situation. I appreciate you."

"Don't mention it. You need to know everything that you're dealing with. The good, the bad, and the ugly, right?"

"Right."

"We'd better get back to the men. Here comes Antonio, I'm sure to check on Daria and Samantha. They've got the little ladies under control."

"Yes, it certainly looks that way."

Chantel and Keisha headed back to their husbands who were engaged in deep conversation.

"Hey, babe. You ladies okay?"

"Yes, I've been getting to know Chantel. We're great."

"I invited them to meet us for dinner the next time they're in DC."

"Yes, Chantel and I were just discussing the same thing. That would be great."

"You ladies hungry? Darius and I were just about to head over to grab a couple of plates. Why don't you find a table and we'll bring you both something," said Chris.

"He's a great guy. It's good to see that you made it through your trials early in the marriage. It gives me great hope."

"You're going to be fine. You're going to make it through all of this and one day when you're both old and grey, you'll realize you made it and you're so much stronger because of it."

Antonio and Samantha headed toward the table with Daria and Keyana.

"Darius went to get us some food. I'm sure they're probably both hungry by now."

"Samantha and I were going to head over to do the same thing. We'll be right back."

Daria and Keyana sat in chairs next to each other laughing at nothing. Before long, the group was enjoying the food and engaging in more conversation. Some about business and some very personal. Samantha took the girls inside to lay them down for a nap. They were both obviously wiped out.

"Antonio, Samantha seems to be quite smitten with you. What are you going to do?" Chantel was not one to hold her tongue when she had something to say.

"We're working through it."

"Don't let her get away, man. She's good with Daria and obviously cares a great deal about you. You'd be a fool to let her go," said Chris.

"Trust me. I've already thought about it. You're right. She's a good lady. I'm just trying to take things slow. I mean, Stephanie was her cousin and all."

"You're right, but Stephanie's gone. Samantha is here helping you pick up the pieces. I believe she's here for a reason, and that reason is to love you. You can't help who you love. Remember that."

"Antonio, no one will judge you if you decide to get involved with her. It's nobody's business but your own," Darius offered.

"Darius is right. I really like her a lot. She's so good with Daria. With both of them. She cares a lot about your well-being and the baby. I mean, look at how much time she's spending with Keyana? She's an amazing woman." Keisha looked at Antonio, then at Chantel.

"Well, you'll figure out what to do," said Chantel. "We'll leave it alone for now."

Antonio already knew what he wanted to do. He wanted to spend his life with Samantha. He knew that his friends were right. You can't help who you love. His family wouldn't be in a position to judge, considering his father was married to one of his dearest friend's ex-mistress. It was Samantha and Stephanie's family that concerned him. What would their mothers have to say about all of this? Should he really care? He really didn't need them for anything. Besides, if Samantha's mother and aunt really loved her, they would just make the best of the situation for the sake of Daria, at least. That's what everyone else was doing.

38 UNTIL NEXT TIME

Keisha, Darius, and Keyana arrived at the airport two hours before departure time. That would give them enough time to return the rental car and get checked in.

"Where's Da-ya?" Keyana asked.

"Daria is with Antonio. You'll see her again soon, okay?" Darius said.

"Wow. She's asking for her already," Keisha shook her head.

"Yes, I figured that would be the case after watching how they got along this weekend."

"Well, it's a good thing they're coming to town next month. It's a good thing we can fly down there for free and Antonio has opened his home to us for future visits. That way, we can go as often as necessary while the two of you work this thing out."

"Yes, that is a good thing. We'll have to do the same when he brings her to town. They'll just have to stay with us. How do you feel about that?"

"Darius, I wouldn't have it any other way. We've got plenty of room. Maybe he'll bring Samantha with him."

"I believe he'll definitely be bringing Samantha with him. We talked again last night after you went to bed. He said he was going to go for it after the conversation we all had with him over dinner yesterday. He loves her. I can tell. Oh, yeah. Before I forget. I asked him to think about joining us on the ski trip in a few weeks, too. I figured he could bring her with him. Maybe my parents wouldn't mind watching both Daria and Keyana while we're gone."

"You know what? I hadn't thought about that, but it's actually a good idea." Keisha admitted. "They can get a chance to get to know her and Keyana will enjoy having her around. This was a very interesting trip, wasn't it? I'm so glad we went. I really enjoyed meeting Chantel and Chris, also. I'm actually looking forward to spending more time with them."

"Yes, they're great people. They have a lot of insight and offered some encouraging words for our marriage and this whole situation. We were supposed to meet them for a reason. Keisha, I really think I'm leaning toward letting Daria stay down there in Atlanta. They can visit us whenever they want, but I don't want to disrupt her life. She seems so happy there. What do you think?"

"Honey, I told you I would support whatever decision you made. What about Keyana, though? What about the two of them developing a great sisterhood? Darius, I've prayed about it and whatever decision you make; I'm okay with it. Just be sure that you think it through thoroughly so that you'll have no regrets."

"If Antonio and Samantha decide to go skiing, we can talk more about it at that time. In the meantime, I'll think about it some more."

"That's probably a good idea. We'll let the dust settle from our visit. I just don't want you to make a hasty decision. You are her father. If you can live with letting him raise her with you sort of waiting on the sideline, that's up to you. Either way, she'll have a great life and will be with people who love and care about her. That's all I have to say about it."

The family was back at home safely within a few hours.

"Thank God for direct flights," said Darius.

"Yes, I couldn't agree more. I'm so tired. I'm going to put Keyana down for a nap. Are you hungry?"

"I don't want you to cook. I'll run back out and pick up something. Maybe a couple of lobsters. What do you think?"

"Sounds delicious."

"I think I'm going to stay home another day. We both could use some rest."

Darius headed to the seafood market while Keisha prepared Keyana for her nap. He dialed Jamel's number.

"Hey, man. It's Darius. Have I got a story for you."

"We were thinking about heading over there. You guys up for some company? We won't stay long."

"I was just about to pick up a couple of lobsters. You guys have plans for dinner?"

"No, we hadn't thought about anything yet."

"Well, come on over. We can talk when you get here."

"Sounds good, man. We'll see you in about an hour. Do you need us to bring anything?"

"No, just yourselves and your appetites. I'll take care of everything else.

"Cool."

39 DINNER WITH FRIENDS

The doorbell rang just as Darius was removing the six lobsters from the lobster pot.

"Keisha, I am so glad to see you," Monica hugged her friend.

"We had a great trip, but I'm glad to be home. Antonio has some nice friends down there. He has a huge support system."

Jamel kissed Keisha's cheek before heading into the kitchen to help Darius.

"So, how was everything?"

"Girl, I don't even know where to begin."

"The beginning is probably the best place. So, tell me about this mansion you stayed in."

"Well, Antonio is really living a good life down there. He lives in a huge house in a very plush neighborhood. The house sits on several acres of land. He's surrounded by doctors, lawyers, a few people in the music industry, actors, actresses. That type scene."

"Okay, okay. Let me find out Antonio is loaded."

"He actually is, Monica. It's weird because he's very down to earth. He hasn't let the money change him, but after meeting his dad I can tell; he comes from money. What he's made from his business is just an added bonus. His father was a little snobbish, but Antonio is very cool and laid back."

"Go on."

"His father is married to a woman who is probably more than ten years younger than him. He's got a trophy wife who actually had an affair with Antonio's good friend several years ago when him and his wife were temporarily separated."

"What?"

"Yes! And they were all at the party together like it was cool. His friend, Chris; the one who had the affair has the coolest wife in the world. You'll meet them in a few months because they're coming to town on business. She's an attorney down there. Her name's Chantel."

"You mean, she's okay with the mistress being around her husband?"

"Yes! She's very confident. You'll see. She said the chick was a gold digger and because her new husband has so much money, she knew she didn't have a thing to worry about. Chantel is very pretty anyway. She's successful in her own right, so she has all the confidence in the world. She had a lot to say about what's going on with Darius and Antonio but get this."

"Girl, you better go ahead. Do I need to pop some popcorn?"

"Samantha, the nanny is actually Stephanie's first cousin."

"What the, what?"

"Yes, she's Stephanie's cousin and she admitted she's in love with Antonio. She's been there taking care of Daria since Stephanie died. Also, according to Chantel; Stephanie had more issues than we knew about. She was abusive to Antonio on more than one occasion."

"Wow!"

"Anyway, that's it."

"So, when is Daria coming to live here?"

"Oh, I forgot that part. Girl, Darius sounds like he might be leaning toward letting her stay down there. I suggested that he think about it some more before making the final decision.

She's thriving down there with him. I get that, but I just don't want to end up on some talk show fifteen or twenty years from now dealing with a young lady who is resentful because she thinks her real father didn't want her. You know what I mean?"

"Yeah, I hear you. After we spoke the other day, I wondered if that might be the case, though. Antonio sounds like he's been doing a great job with her. Better than a lot of biological dads we've known over the years. Some of them never even contact them at all. Think about it."

"That's for sure. You know something else, though? Samantha is so good with her. She was good with Keyana too. I would have no problem letting Keyana go down there to spend some time with her sister when she gets a little older. Samantha was just that great."

"Well, let me meet this Samantha chick before you go sending my goddaughter down to Atlanta, okay?"

"Deal," Keisha laughed.

"Ladies, come on. It's time to eat."

Both couples enjoyed dinner while engaging in more conversation about the trip. They would get a chance to meet Samantha, Antonio, Chris, and Chantel before long. Monica was very protective of Keisha and Keyana and the fact that Samantha was Stephanie's cousin put her on high alert. She would have to wait and see.

"I'm just glad you're home. I missed you, my friend. I'll have to fill you in on the wedding plans. I think I found my dress!"

"That's great news, Monica! I can't wait to see it."

"I'm glad you feel that way because I made an appointment at the bridal shop for Thursday evening and I was hoping you could go with me."

"I wouldn't miss it for anything in the world."

"Can you believe it's almost time for our ski trip?"

"No, the time sure flew by. I can't wait to get out there and have some fun in the snow."

"You may get an opportunity to meet Samantha and

Antonio during that weekend. Darius invited them."

"What in the world? Well, alright then. He must really like that dude."

"Well, that dude is raising his daughter and loving her just like she was his own."

"You're right. I'm sorry I'm being so judgmental about all of this. It's a lot to take in. Anyway, when we get back, I'm going to have to focus most of my attention on the wedding plans."

"Yes, you and me both. I'm available for whatever you need. Don't forget that."

"I know you are. I'm so excited."

"I'm happy for you. Just think, you're almost a married woman."

"Yes, and I owe a lot of it to you. If it weren't for you, I would never have met the man of my dreams."

"Monica, I truly believe you two would have met somehow without me. Jamel is meant for you."

"Yes, he is." Monica stared at the love of her life from across the table. She loved him so much and couldn't believe they would be married soon. They were both disciplined and still had not engaged in any sexual activity. They were waiting until their wedding night, and she was so glad they were.

40 BLACK PEOPLE DON'T SKI

The group arrived at the cabin just as the snow began to fall. The ground was already covered with six inches, which made a good foundation for the four or five inches they were expecting.

"Thank God for four-wheel drive," said Darius.

"What time are Cynthia and Terrence supposed to get here? I sure hope they make it before this snow gets any worse."

"They should be here any minute. I spoke to him just before we left, and they were about to get on the road then."

"I'm so glad things are working out for those too. They both deserve to be happy."

"You've got that right. Antonio and Samantha should be here in a couple of hours, too. Dad called to say they'd already gotten them from the airport. He took them to pick up the rental car before heading back to the house with Keyana and Daria."

"That really was a great idea. The girls are going to have so much fun together."

"The girls? Mom and Dad are gonna have a blast. They've been waiting to meet Daria, and you know Keyana's been excited since we told her she was coming. I'm just looking forward to spending some time with our grown and sexy friends. We've got quite a weekend planned."

"Babe, how about we take this room? It's got a huge bathroom with a soaking tub. What do you think?"

"Yeah, it's nice. Three of the other rooms have soaking tubs, too. The agent said there were two smaller rooms that share a bathroom. So, everybody should get pretty decent quarters."

"Sounds like Jamel and Monica might have picked the room at the end of the hall. The one that overlooks the backyard and the hot tub. We're gonna make a run to the store. Where's the list?"

"Babe, please don't forget the salmon. I need it for tonight's dinner," she handed him the list.

Each couple would take a day to prepare the meals for everyone. It was something Darius came up with after Chef Jacques's wife came down with the flu and he had to cancel.

"I got you, babe. I won't forget anything," he scanned the list. "What are we making tonight?"

"I'm gonna try out this salmon casserole recipe that Helena gave me. It sounds delicious."

"Alright, babe. We'll be right back." He kissed Keisha on the cheek before heading down the hall. "Jamel, man; you ready?"

"Let's go, let's go!" Jamel kissed Monica, grabbed his wallet and headed out the door just as Cynthia and Terrence were pulling into the driveway.

"Hey, man! You wanna roll with us? Cynthia, the ladies are in the house. We can bring the suitcases in when we get back."

"Hi, Darius. Yeah, that sounds good. I'll see you in a bit, babe," Terence escorted her to the door. "Do you need anything?"

"I don't know. Maybe a bottle of white wine or something? How about some Moscato?"

"Okay, I got it. Love you."

"I love you too."

"Man, you're already up to the L word? Things must be going pretty good between you too," Darius joked.

"Yeah, I would say that. She's a special lady. I can see myself marrying her someday. Man, you should see her with Ashley and Aliyah. She's definitely a nurturer. I'm surprised she doesn't have any kids of her own."

"I don't know, man. If you marry her, how is Erica gonna feel about that? And the fact that she'll have direct access to the girls?"

"I don't care how she feels about it. I've already told her that she better get used to it anyway. She had her chance."

"Well, I'm glad things are going well for you. Both of you deserve some happiness."

Darius pulled into the grocery store parking lot.

"What in the world? Antonio and Samantha! What are you guys doing here? When did you get into town?"

"We literally just pulled in. Sam wanted to pick up what we needed for tomorrow," Antonio and Darius slapped hands.

"Man, I want you to meet my boy, Jamel. Jamel, this is Antonio. This is Terrence. He's a buddy of mine from work. Oh, and this is his lady; Samantha."

"It's nice to meet all of you," she said. Samantha was a little shy. Perhaps an introvert, but there was more confidence in there than she would ever admit.

"Babe, I'll head into the store to grab these items if you want to stay with your friends."

"Okay, we'll be right in."

"That's a good lady, right there," Darius said.

"Yes, she is. She's a keeper."

"So, you finally got over the fact Stephanie was her cousin?"

"I'm over it. Her mother gave her blessings. That's all that matters, although I would have still pursued it if she'd been against it. I've learned that you can't please everybody," he admitted.

"You've got that right, so you might as well be happy and

don't worry about what others have to say."

"We'd better get in there. This snow is really coming down. Keisha's got everything but the kitchen sink on this list."

The fellas headed into the store to finish the shopping before heading back to the cabin.

"Babe! We're back! Guess who I found?"

"Samantha, I'm so glad to see you." The two women embraced. "Let me introduce you to everyone. First, I want you to meet my best friend, Monica. Monica, this is Samantha."

"Well, it's nice to finally meet you. Keisha has been raving about you since she returned from Atlanta," Monica admitted.

"I've heard so much about you, too. It's a pleasure to meet you."

"This is Cynthia. She's another dear friend."

"It's nice to meet you, Samantha."

"It's nice to meet you, too."

"So, did you guys have a good flight? What did you think about Darius's parents?"

"We had a great flight, although Daria wasn't too thrilled about being on the plane."

"Awe, poor baby!"

"Yeah, she was a little restless. Darius's parents are great. By the time we reached the airport and Daria saw Keyana, she didn't care about us at all. She wasn't even upset that we were leaving her."

"They're going to have a great time. Don't worry about her. She's in great hands," Keisha said, realizing that this was the first time the baby didn't have at least one of them with her.

"If you all haven't chosen a room already, you might want to go ahead and do that. We've got some surprise guests who should be arriving any minute," Darius yelled.

"Surprise guests? Darius, what are you talking about?"

"Didn't I just say it was a surprise, babe?"

"What is he talking about?"

Monica shrugged her shoulders.

"I guess I better get dinner started, then."

"You want us to help you? I have a feeling that we got railroaded anyway. You know they have no intentions on cooking a single thing while we're here," Monica laughed.

"You're probably right. Sure, I guess I could use a hand."

"Hey!" Yelled a familiar voice from the front door.

"Shawn! What are you doing here? Hey, Tyrone," Keisha hugged Shawn tightly around the neck.

"Hey, y'all! Did Pam get here yet?"

"Pam? She's coming too? Oh my God, I haven't seen you guys in a good while!" Monica said.

"Hey, Monica. Yes, Pam and her boo will be here soon. You know she's been dating one of the ministers from church."

"I'd heard that, but I wasn't sure. I haven't seen her since she started attending the second service. We always go to the first one."

"That's why she started going the second service. It's because of him."

Monica chuckled, "Some things never change."

"What are you talking about?"

"Girl, you know something about everything and everybody, don't you?"

"You got that right. If I don't stay in the know, then you won't know."

"So, when did you and Tyrone get back together? Tell that!" Monica yelled.

"We've been back together since we got back from St. Thomas. We'll talk about that later."

"Alright, now," Monica said. "I'm glad you guys worked it all out."

"Shawn, there's one room left with a King-sized bed. I'm assuming that's the one you and Tyrone will take. Pam and Minister Steve can take the other two rooms with the Queen-sized beds and the adjoining bathroom. I'm sure they won't mind, considering."

"Pam, with her holier than thou self? She wouldn't have it any other way."

"Shawn, you're still crazy!"

"Anyway, come on over here so you can meet everybody. Looks like Darius has already introduced your husband. Samantha, this is Shawn. She's another one of our friends."

"It's nice to meet you, Shawn."

"Nice to meet you too, who are you?"

"Really, Shawn?"

"We can talk about all of that after dinner. The guys said they were going to shoot a few rounds of pool. This house has a huge game room. Anyway, Antonio is Samantha's man. It's a long story. Please don't ask right now. I promise we'll talk later."

"Girl, you better! Because there are a lot of strange faces all up in this place!"

"Wait a minute. Isn't that Terrence? The one from the FAA?"

"You don't miss much, do you?" Terrence yelled from the family room that overlooked the kitchen.

"You know I don't!"

"Okay, Shawn. Calm your nerves. Terrence and I are seeing each other," said Cynthia. "That's another thing I suppose we'll have to talk about later."

"Girl! Where have I been? I go away for a little while to bring my family back together, and there's a whole lot of love connections that I missed!"

"This girl is a fool," Monica whispered, "but it wouldn't be a party without her, would it?"

"That's for sure," Keisha agreed.

"Pam! Hey!" Shawn yelled.

"Get on in here with the Bishop!"

"Shawn, he is not a bishop. Stop playing, now."

"Hey, everybody!"

Keisha introduced Pam and Minister Steve to the people they hadn't met.

"Wow! This is going to be the best ski weekend ever! The

gang's all here!"

"Yes, we're gonna have some fun alright. Hanging around this cabin, because y'all know black people don't ski!"

Everyone burst into laughter. Shawn had always been the life of the party, and although she hadn't been around in a while; she still was.

41 WHO AM I TO JUDGE?

"Samantha, please tell Helena I said thanks for that salmon recipe. It was absolutely delicious!"

"You're welcome. I'm glad everyone enjoyed it."

"I guess we can take over the family room since the guys are headed to the game room."

"So, what in the world has been going on?" Shawn inquired as she scanned the ladies' faces.

"Girl, so much. Where do you wanna start?"

"First of all. Monica, how are the wedding plans going?"

"They're going great. Thanks for asking."

"Okay, so it looks like Monica and Jamel are drama free. On to the next. Samantha, where are you from?"

"We came up from Atlanta."

"Shawn, you don't play, do you?" Keisha asked.

"Samantha is Antonio's girlfriend."

"Okay, you already said that, but I don't even know who Antonio is. This is my first time seeing him."

"Alright. Here goes. Antonio was Stephanie's boyfriend, and now he's with Samantha."

"Wait. Stephanie? Wasn't she Darius's crazy ex-girlfriend? The one Monica . . . never mind."

"Stephanie was Darius's friend. She was actually

dating Antonio. Okay, it turns out that Darius and Stephanie had a daughter. Antonio's been taking care of her."

"Wait a minute! What are you talking about?"

"Shawn, you better listen because I'm never repeating this story again. Pam, you too. Not long after Keyana was born, Antonio showed up at our house with a little girl that he thought was his daughter. According to Stephanie, she was anyway. It turns out that Antonio wasn't her father, but Darius is."

"What? That's some bull!"

"Shawn, just shut up and listen," said Pam.

"Okay, okay. I'm listening."

"Anyway, Darius didn't know about Daria, his daughter; but he's the father. The DNA test confirmed it."

"Wow! This is crazy! So, Samantha; where did you come from? How do you fit into this love triangle? Actually, it's a love square. Now, this is some mess right here."

"Antonio and I weren't dating during that time. He hired me to help him with Daria after my cousin died. We just recently started dating."

"Oh, okay. I'm sorry to hear about your cousin."

"Okay, so after Stephanie died; Samantha started helping out and the two of them have since fallen in love."

"Wait, Stephanie who? Stephanie? Stephanie?"

"Yes, Stephanie, Stephanie. Shawn, please follow," Keisha was getting frustrated.

"Shawn, listen! Stephanie and Samantha were cousins. Do you understand the words that are coming out of Keisha's mouth? Dang!" Pam was now frustrated too.

"What? This is some mess right here," she shook her head in disbelief. "You know what, though? Who am I to judge? We've all had family drama in one way or another.

Keisha, are you and Darius okay?"

"Yes, we're fine. We're taking it one day at a time, but we're getting through it."

"Okay, if you're good. I'm good. She offered Keisha a hug. "You know I love you, girl. Oh, and Samantha; please forgive me. I was just trying to understand this whole thing. I hope I didn't offend you."

"No, I'm fine. I totally understand. It is a lot to take in."

"Well, after what I went through with my own husband? Nothing surprises me anymore. I just need to learn how to mind my own business. Shoot, you ask a lot of questions; you might be surprised by the answers. Y'all surely surprised me with this news."

"Enough about all that. Can we change the subject?" Pam asked.

"Sure Pam, what you got?"

"Steve asked me to marry him!" She held her left hand up.

"Oh my God! Congratulations! I am truly happy for you two," Keisha's eyes filled with tears. "Look at God! Won't He do it?"

"Yes, He will!" Pam was beaming from ear to ear as she became extra excited about her future.

42 TEMPTATION

"Today looks like a great day to go snowmobiling, but whose idea was it for the ladies to go separately from the fellas?"

"Shawn, you know how Darius is. He said we would slow him down, so we have two separate instructors. We'll be out there at the same time. Just in two separate groups."

"Well, whatever. I'm just ready to have some fun. Tyrone bought me this new ski suit and snow boots. I'm ready to put my new outfit to good use."

"Come on everybody! It's time to go! The van is out here!" Keisha yelled.

"Keisha, I can't find my phone. You guys go ahead. I'll just drive out there to meet you in a few minutes."

Darius searched the family room sofa cushions for his phone. There was nothing.

"What did I do with that thing?"

He ran upstairs to check the bedroom again. Still nothing.

"Maybe I left it in the game room last night?"

He ran down to the game room, but the phone couldn't be found anywhere. He opened the cabinet. His heart began to race. He hadn't been in the presence of liquor in quite a while and there staring back at him were bottles of Ciroc in every flavor. He picked up one of the bottles and held it tightly in his hand. Then he placed it back gently in line with the others and walked away.

"Where is that phone? Come on now."

"Pick it up."

Darius looked around the room. Certain he was there alone, he had no idea where the voice came from.

"Pick it up."

There it was again.

He opened the cabinet and picked up the bottle of Red Berry Ciroc. Staring at it for a while, he unscrewed the top. The aroma was something that he'd been so used to at one time in his life, but it was so foreign now. He put the bottle under his nose and inhaled.

"What am I doing?"

He inhaled it again.

"Take a sip," said the voice.

Darius scanned the room again. There was no one there.

"You know you want it."

He heard the voice behind him. It was getting closer.

Meanwhile, Keisha, Monica, and Samantha engaged in a race on their snowmobiles while Pam and Shawn trailed a short distance behind. The guys were racing like there was a check waiting at the end the finish line for them. They were having a great time. Keisha wondered what was taking Darius so long, so she pulled over and turned her snowmobile off. After four rings, the phone went to voicemail.

"Darius, it's me. What's taking you so long? Call me back."

"You okay?" Monica yelled as her snowmobile came to rest alongside Keisha's.

"I was trying to get Darius. He's not answering, though."

"I'm sure he's on his way. You know he wouldn't leave you out here for too long without him."

"Yeah, you're probably right."

"If he doesn't show in a few minutes, I'll have the driver take us back to make sure he's okay."

"Okay."

"I think I better head back. The others should stay. I don't want to ruin their fun."

"I'll go with you. I'm not letting you go by yourself."

"The driver will watch out for me, I'm fine."

"No, I'm not leaving you. Let me just tell Jamel that I'm running back with you. Be right back."

"What's going on? Why is the car still here?" Keisha asked as the van pulled up to the house.

"Girl, I don't know. I know he's not still looking for that phone!"

"Darius!" Keisha yelled after wiping her snow-covered boots on the carpet in the entryway. "Darius! Where are you?"

"I'll check upstairs, Monica said. "Darius?"

Keisha looked out the window in the backyard. Darius wasn't there.

"Babe! Where are you?" She headed down to the game room.

"Oh my God! Monica! Help me! Monica!"

Monica raced down the stairs to where her friend was kneeling on the floor.

"Oh my God! What happened?"

"Call 911, please! Call 911! Darius, baby! What's wrong?"

"Hello, please send an ambulance to 633 Snow Mountain Road! Please hurry. My friend is unconscious on the floor!"

"Please stay with me. Can you check his pulse?"

"Keisha, check his pulse."

"Yes, he has a pulse but he's not responding to me!"

Monica picked up the empty bottle of Ciroc that was lying at his feet.

"Darius, no! Please, no!" Monica sobbed.

"Keisha, I'm so sorry. I'm so sorry."

Keisha looked at the empty bottle as tears poured uncontrollably down her face.

"Please hurry!"

"The ambulance is already on route, Ma'am. Please stay with me."

Monica held Keisha who was on the floor holding Darius in her arms.

"Baby, why?" Why?" She cried.

"I hear the ambulance!" Monica ran upstairs to let the paramedics in.

"He's downstairs!"

"I'm going to ride with him! Here are the keys, Oh my God! I can't believe this is happening!"

The ambulance raced toward the hospital as fast as it could considering the slippery road conditions.

"Jamel! I need you!"

"What's going on, babe?"

"We're on our way to the hospital! When we got back to the house, we found Darius passed out on the basement floor! He drank a whole bottle of Ciroc! Please get here as soon as you can. I don't even know the name of the hospital in this town, but please hurry!"

"Okay, okay. Calm down. We're on our way!"

They found Monica consoling Keisha in the waiting area when they arrived at the hospital.

"What's going on? Is he okay?"

"Babe, I don't know. They're trying to stabilize him. They said we had to wait out here."

Jamel grabbed Keisha and held her in his arms. She could barely stand up on her own.

"It's okay. It's okay."

Jamel wasn't sure that it would be, but he tried to sound convincing. They had been through so much, he wasn't sure if they could survive this. He vowed to never take a drink again, but here he was in what was probably an alcohol induced coma.

"Mrs. Kingston?"

"Yes?" Keisha began to tremble as she stood to greet the doctor.

"Hello, I'm Dr. Meyer."

"Hi, Dr. Meyer. What's wrong with my husband?"

"We've gotten him stable. You should be able to see him in a couple of minutes. It's a good thing you found him when you did."

"Dr. Meyer, can you tell me what his blood alcohol level is? It looks like he drank the whole bottle."

"Excuse me?"

"There was an empty Ciroc bottle on the floor next to him. My husband is a recovering alcoholic," Keisha sobbed.

"Mrs. Kingston, there was no alcohol in your husband's system."

"What? But the bottle was empty."

"No, Ma'am. There was no alcohol in his system."

"It looks like he just passed out. That's it. You might want to talk to him, though; because he's rambling a very odd story in there."

"Can I see him?"

Keisha followed Dr. Meyer to the ER room where Darius was resting on a stretcher.

"Babe. Oh, my God. I thought . . ."

"Hey, baby. I'm okay."

"Darius, what happened?"

"Keisha, I was looking for my phone. I looked all over the house and couldn't find it. I went down to the game room, thinking I'd left it down there last night; but it wasn't there. I don't know what prompted me to do it, but I saw the cabinet and when I opened it, it was full of liquor."

"Babe, there was an empty bottle on the floor. I thought you had relapsed."

"No, babe. I'll admit, I did take the top off, but the smell of it . . . Keisha, the smell of it disgusted me. Then I heard a voice. It was a whisper. The voice told me to take a sip. I heard the voice as clear as you can hear me talking to you right now. When I turned around, she was there."

"Darius, who was there?"

"The voice. The voice told me to pick up the bottle and

take a sip. She told me to drink it."

"Darius, who are you talking about?"

"Keisha, it was Stephanie. I could see her standing there, telling me to take a sip. Then I passed out. I must have dropped the bottle when I hit the floor."

"Babe, Stephanie is dead. Remember? She's dead."

"Babe, I know that; but she . . . her spirit or something was standing there. She told me to drink. She's still trying to destroy me. Even in death."

"Darius, don't say that. We'll talk about that later. I'm just glad you're okay. I'm so glad you didn't listen," Keisha continued to sob.

"Baby, I told you I would never drink again. The love I have for you means that much to me. I would never jeopardize what we have by going back to that life. Never. I love you so much, Keisha."

"Baby, I love you too."

Monica and Jamel walked into the room.

"Is he gonna be okay?"

"Yes, he is. He didn't do it. He didn't do it, Monica. He didn't drink it."

"I know, I heard the doctor."

"He said Stephanie was there. She was telling him to take a drink," Keisha whispered.

"What?"

"Yes, he said he saw her spirit. He thinks she's haunting him. Still trying to destroy him."

"You'll have to get him some help. He's probably suffering from some sort of anxiety. Keisha, a lot has happened."

"Mrs. Kinston, we're going to let you take your husband home in a little while. I'm just waiting for the rest of his labs to come back, but so far everything looks good. As soon as I get the last report, I'll sign the release. I do suggest that you get him some counseling, though. His story is a little unbelievable."

"Yes, Dr. Meyer. I'll see to it that he gets the help he

needs. You can't even imagine the stuff we've been through lately. It's no wonder he's seeing and hearing things. I probably should get some counseling too, but one thing's for sure. Love endures all things. I can't express that enough. We're going to be okay."

Keisha stayed with Darius until the nurse returned with is release papers. In fact, the entire group of friends waited. They would continue their ski vacation back at the cabin just enjoying each other the way friends do. Keisha was so thankful that he hadn't given in to the temptation of the alcohol. It takes a strong person to say no, but he'd made a promise and it was his intention to keep it for the rest of their lives.

PART III

(A SNEAK PEEK)

Monica looked at her reflection in the mirror. The day had finally arrived.

"You look absolutely amazing, my friend. I'm so happy for you."

"Keisha, you better not make me cry. You'll have to do my makeup again and I haven't even made it down the aisle."

"Girl, we've been through some things, haven't we?"

"Yes, we have; but I'm so glad I had you to go through it all with. I wouldn't change a thing. Look at how much we've grown. How much we've matured."

"You're right. They were all life lessons."

"We look good in these dresses!"

"Shawn, you got that right. We do look good," Pam agreed.

"Well, we'd better get ready. It's time to do this. You ready?"

"Am I ready? I'm about to marry the man God created just for me. Yes, I'm ready!"

"Let's go, then."

Samantha and Pam grabbed the back of the six-foot train on Monica's beautiful gown. The ladies headed out of the dressing area and into the church lobby where they awaited their cues from the wedding planner.

"Wow, man. Look at your bride," Darius whispered in Jamel's ear.

"She looks amazing," Jamel wiped the tear that was resting in the corner of his right eye. "I can't believe this day has finally arrived."

"Baby girl, you look beautiful," Toni said after raising the veil from his daughter's face before handing her over to Jamel. He kissed her on the cheek before taking his place next to Tonya.

"Dearly beloved, we are gathered here today to join this man and this woman in holy matrimony," said the pastor.

Monica stared into Jamel's eyes. She smiled.

"This union will not be entered into lightly," he continued until he'd reached the end of the opening words.

"Hold up," Darius said to himself as he looked over the crowd of their friends and families.

Monica and Jamel hadn't noticed because they were exchanging their personal dedications to one another.

Tyrone discreetly left his seat and headed toward the back of the church. He had noticed him too.

"You may kiss the bride," the pastor said.

Monica and Jamel were already engaged in a very long and intimate kiss before the pastor could finish. They faced the crowd as they were introduced as Mr. and Mrs. Jamel Martin.

"We did it, babe! We're married," Monica couldn't contain her excitement. As the couple headed back up the aisle toward the exit doors.

"Oh my God! What are you doing here?" Monica stopped dead in her tracks.

Tyrone had him pinned against the wall. He was holding him like his life and the lives of everyone else in the room depended on it.

"I spotted him a few minutes ago," said Tyrone. "Jamel, you guys get out of here. I'll take care of it."

Jamel grabbed Monica's hand as the wedding party headed toward the limos.

"Oh my God, Jamel. Where did he come from?" she asked.

"I don't know, but there's no need for you to worry. Tyrone said he'd handle it, and he will." He looked back at Darius for reassurance.

In the back of his mind, he wondered what was going on but was certain PG County PD was on it. He could hear the sirens getting closer.

"It's okay, honey. It's okay," he rubbed the back of her head as she buried her face into his chest. "Let's just get to the reception and have a good time. We'll be out of here first thing in the morning headed for Paris. No need for you to trouble yourself with any of this."

Jamel knew he wouldn't let anyone harm Monica. They had come so far. Someone would have to answer to this. How had Rico managed to get out of prison? What was he doing there? He was determined to ruin their wedding day, but Jamel would ensure that it didn't happen. By any means necessary.

ABOUT THE AUTHOR

Terri Seymore-Green, originally of Southampton, NY; currently resides in Prince George's County, MD. *Love Endures All Things* is the sequel to *I Love You More Than Love*. Formerly, she was an analyst specializing in projects and process improvements and writing technical procedures. Today, she enjoys writing books, promoting her work, and engaging with her followers through her blog.

Please check her out at www.terriseymoregreen.com. She can be reached by email at terriseymoregreen@gmail.com, or in writing at Poetry and Prose II, 15912-B Crain Hwy Suite 308, Brandywine, MD 20613. She would love to hear your thoughts.

PAGE INTENTIONALLY LEFT BLANK.